TALISMAN MOUNTAIN TRILOGY BOOK ONE

SAMANTHA THOMAS

First edition published 2019
All production design are trademarks of Samantha Thomas.

For information regarding bulk purchases of this book, digital purchase and special discounts, please contact the author

Editing provided by Kerrie McLoughlin
Formatting and cover provided by Suzette Vaughn

CHAPTER ONE

Still clenching the steering wheel with a white-knuckled grip, Alex Mason took another deep breath. The car's engine was still running, but she wouldn't be driving anywhere soon.

The deer had come out of nowhere. She had been lucky she missed the animal, but now she was stuck, the front end of her rental nose deep in the snow banks lining the icy road to Talisman Mountain.

Alex turned off her music. She looked down at her phone, not surprised there wasn't any service available. Not that she had anyone to call out here. She hadn't been back in nearly 16 years. It was only her father's death that had forced her to make the trip.

She had received the notification from Cal Stenson, her father's business partner. Cal had been sympathetic when he delivered the news, but there were no words to erase the guilt she felt. She should have spent more time with her father. She should have returned to Talisman sooner. Her father had come to visit her in the city, but Alex had not been to his place at the resort in years. This was not how she had planned on returning. With the loss of her father, she hadn't planned on returning at all.

Alex had been angry when Cal informed her the funeral had already happened. It had been a low-key affair, as per her father's wishes; he didn't want Alex to feel pressured to come back. Not after everything that had happened.

Alex gave her head a shake. She didn't need to revisit those memories. Right now, she needed to get out of this bloody car and to the chalet. If memory served correctly, it was less than a mile ahead. Close enough to walk.

Alex rubbed at the fogged window; the snow was still blowing outside, and she was reminded how cold the walk to the resort was going to be. She twisted to grab her bag from the back seat. She would have to make sure she was well dressed for the hike ahead. Frostbite was the last thing she needed to add to her list of problems. Alex pulled the warm balaclava over her head and zipped up her fluorescent pink down jacket. If another vehicle came down the same road, she would be seen instantly. She had on so many layers, Alex was worried she was going to get stuck in the cramped seat.

Alex was still irritated with the rental company. She tried to explain to the agent that a sports car would be less than ideal for her journey. Well, maybe it was more that she yelled at him, but dealing with people had never been Alex's strong suit. She preferred numbers, simple, uncomplicated, black and white numbers. She calculated her chances of changing the mind of Doug, the YouTube video-watching agent, as unlikely and accepted the two-door coupe. She didn't want to waste any more time. Bad choice.

Mentally preparing for the cold, Alex pushed open the door and stepped out into the biting wind. With a better view, she could see there was no damage, just a prison of snow. She was definitely going to need to be pulled out. She heard the beep as she locked the door, then she laughed aloud. It was doubtful that anyone would be out looking to steal a car in this weather. Perhaps she had been in the city too long.

Despite the circumstance, Alex could appreciate the walk. The snow had dampened any sound, so that all she could hear was the crunching of her boots on the road. Alex couldn't remember the last time she had been surrounded by silence. Work was always a cacophony of phones and interruptions, and the city, even asleep, had the hum of a machine that never shut off.

Alex was surprised at how good it felt. Snow-capped trees, branches drooping from the weight of the recent fall, and sparkling flakes dancing as they fell. It was a pretty picture. She stuck out her tongue to catch some of the fat snowflakes. When was the last time she had enjoyed that simple pleasure?

The low rumble of an engine prevented her from answering that question. Alex turned back the way she had come. She lifted her hand to flag the truck down and started back to her rental.

The truck pulled alongside her trapped car and stopped. Even through the swirling snow the headlights were bright, and Alex couldn't see who was inside. It was a moment or two before the driver jumped out, followed by a large dog. The stranger bent down next to her tire, pushing away some of the snow while the dog padded over to greet her.

The man stood up as she arrived, and she was met with a pair of striking blue eyes and snowflake-kissed lashes. It was all she could see, as he had also covered his face against the freezing cold.

'She's definitely stuck. There's no way you're driving it out.'

He was certainly friendly enough. Alex was hopeful she could remove potential serial killer off her list of concerns.

'I know. I thought the resort was close enough I could walk and get help.' Alex hoped her estimation had been right; for some strange reason, she was concerned this complete stranger would think her a fool.

His eyebrows lifted in surprise. 'You're right, still a bit of a hike, but you would have made it.' The stranger appeared to give her a once-over with those blue eyes. ‘You’re dressed for it.’ He gave a little chuckle.

The man was teasing her! Alex was glad her face was covered, otherwise he would have seen the blush rise to her cheeks. She could play this game too.

‘Would you have preferred I was underdressed?’ Alex paused, ‘For this weather, I mean.’

He didn’t even hesitate in his response. ‘Do you have a habit of underdressing…for the weather, I mean?’

‘I believe I’m usually appropriately dressed for the occasion.’

‘Well, the forecast is saying it’s supposed to get warmer. Seems right; I think I can already feel the temperature rising.’

Alex gave a low laugh. The absurdity of it all was quite amusing. She was standing in the middle of the road, flirting with a man she had never met, after ramming her car into a wall of snow. And she liked it.

‘I’d like to offer you a ride into Talisman, but you would only end up seated tightly next to me, as Chewie here likes his spot in the truck and has no clear personal boundaries.’ The stranger gave a nod toward the tail-wagging retriever, as if that would explain it all.

Yes, this man was definitely flirting with her. Alex decided to respond in kind. ‘I’m sure it would be rather cozy—’

‘Easy now, I was only saying that I’d like to. Truth is I have some chains and hooks that should pull you right out of there.’

The man’s interruption would have been a little embarrassing if she hadn’t seen that twinkle in his eyes. Normally she would have been tongue-tied by this point; casual flirtation had never been her thing. But something about this guy was encouraging her to test the waters.

'Oh, thank goodness, that's much more preferable. I would like to get there as soon as possible.'

Alex was pleased by the hint of disappointment that flickered across his brow in response. It didn't last long before the corners of those ridiculously blue eyes were creasing again. It must be the sky-blue scarf he was using to protect his face. It highlighted what were probably regular old eyes into something falsely captivating. She guessed it had been purchased with that in mind. Smart.

'I can't say I'm not disappointed in your choice, but I guess I'm not surprised.'

That caught her off guard.

'What do you mean by that?'

'A Nissan Coupe isn't my idea of a solid choice for the 'I'm going skiing!' crowd.'

'It's a rental!'

'It's a clear sign that today isn't being filled by good decision making on your end. You let me know if you want to fix that track record.' He looked over his shoulder. 'Truck's warm.'

Wow. Alex wasn't sure who had taught this guy to flirt, but he could retake a few lessons. She bent down to pick up one of the hooks he had brought out of the truck.

'Just hook it up, Casanova.' Alex handed him the hook. She could tell he was smiling beneath his gear and found herself smiling back. There was no doubt this guy was a charmer.

'Yes, ma'am. You can go warm up if you like. I've got this.'

He took the hook from her glove, hesitating for a moment. Maybe he was right; Alex was definitely starting to feel hotter in all this clothing. Temperature must be warming up.

Alex bent down next to him, helping attach the chain and hook to her bumper.

'I can help… it'll go faster.'

He gave her a sideways glance. 'What makes you think I want this to go faster?'

Alex shook her head. 'You don't stop, do you?'

'Are you asking me to?' He held up a hand before she could respond. 'Alright, how about this? So… you're not from around here, are you?'

Even that sounded suggestive, and Alex was sure if she were to unwind the scarf that had been wrapped around his face, she would have uncovered a boyish grin.

'Not really.' It was a curt reply, but Alex didn't think he was looking for an in-depth story explaining her return to Talisman Mountain. Besides, she wasn't even sure if she knew the real answer to that question. Was she really 'from' here? After her parents' divorce, Alex had left to live in the city with her mother. There were visits back to see her dad and brother, but after everything had happened, Alex couldn't bring herself to return. Her father had understood that. Too well, maybe. Alex regretted that stubborn insistence now. The stranger seemed to sense she wasn't going to elaborate and didn't push.

'Well, you're going to love it. It's a gorgeous resort, best powder in the world. Best place in the world if you are looking for some R & R.'

'I can see you're a big fan of the place.' Alex gave a small laugh at his favorable description of the resort.

The man spread his arms wide. 'What's not to love? Small crowds, tons of powder, and the best pub for miles!'

'Miles?' Alex gave a skeptical look around.

The man responded with a warm laugh that she could feel all the way through to her toes. 'Yes, miles, don't burst my bubble. In fact, I am very close with the owner. Really great guy, I mean really great. At least that's what absolutely everyone says about him.'

His teasing manner was contagious.

'Really? And how does a man so busy pleasing everyone find time to save fair maidens on the side of the road?'

'A man can always find time for what's important. Damsels in distress usually make the top of the list.'

He gave her a wink as he spoke, and Alex was no longer sure the cold could explain the shiver she felt.

He suddenly stood up and whacked the trunk with his gloved hand. 'There! Let's give it a shot. Hop in and throw it into neutral. Last thing you want is to owe the rental folks a new differential. Once I have you back on the road, you should be good to go.' Once again, he laughed. 'But let me pull those chains off first.'

Alex hesitated, a little sad this chance encounter was ending. It was likely the most pleasant thing her week here was going to entail.

'Well... thank you. I really do appreciate you, and of course Chewie, stopping to help me.'

'Don't thank me yet. Let's see if this works first. If it does, you can thank me by swinging by T-Bar and letting me buy you a drink. Once you're settled in, that is.'

Alex thrust out her thick mitts to shake his hand. 'It's a deal!'

He took her hand. For a moment, it felt as though he was going to pull her in to him. Alex could feel her heart race a little faster, and a flash of pleasure ran through her. They both stood there, hands joined, and blue eyes locked on hazel. The rumble of his truck's engine matched the vibrations running through her entire body. What was going on?

Alex broke their contact and opened the door to her car. 'Thanks again.'

The man nodded. 'My pleasure.'

Alex watched in her side-view mirror as the man and his dog jumped back into their truck. She felt a bit of a jolt as he pulled her out. It matched her reaction to this entire experience. Once she was back safely on the road, the stranger hopped out, throwing the chains and hooks into the bed of the truck.

Alex gave a grateful wave as he drove off.

Smiling, Alex's eyes caught her reflection in the rear-view mirror. That was when she saw her covered face.

No! The realization hit her. Neither one of them had any idea what the other looked like. On top of it, she had been so caught up in their teasing exchange she had forgotten to ask his name. She was going to have to pop into this amazing pub if she hoped to see the helpful stranger again. It shouldn't be too difficult to find the owner of a set of eyes that blue. This week was going to be hard enough as it was. It might be nice to have some friendly company through it all. Alex pushed aside thoughts of the charming stranger. She would have time to indulge in those later.

She pulled off her balaclava, readjusted her thick blonde braid, and rubbed her pink cheeks to warm them up. It would have been impossible to drive in all her layers, so Alex threw the extra gear into the backseat. Once organized, she pointed the front end of her car back down the road. It was time to get to business.

***

Whistling as he drove off, Bohdi Vonn gave the sweet spot behind Chewie's left ear a good scratch.

'Well, that was unexpected, hey, Chew?'

Chewie simply sighed and laid his head to rest on Bohdi's leg. He was agreeable to anything that prompted an ear rub.

Bohdi was feeling pretty good about the day's turn of events. Chewie had received a clean bill of health from Bow Creek's vet and Bohdi had rewarded them both with a donut from the local coffee shop. He had expected a quiet trip back to the hill, but instead found quite the opposite. People were hitting the ditch all the time on their way to the resort. Between wildlife and weather, if you weren't used to winter driving, you were likely to find yourself in trouble. It was usually on the way to the resort. Folks were excited to get started on their vacations, and not always paying attention. It was why he always kept the chains in the back of his truck. This encounter proved how wise it was that he did.

The lady in the ridiculous rental had definitely caught his interest. It had been a long time since anyone had done so. Bohdi knew he was a decent-looking guy. It explained the endorsement offers he had received. An Olympic skier flashing those straight pearly whites can sell toothpaste like nobody's business. Thank goodness it had. Those endorsements had paid for his pub, the T-Bar, and allowed his retreat from the sport. He still garnered some attention for his celebrity, but those relationships always lacked real meaning.

Funny that it was a shapeless parka and assessing hazel eyes that had him hoping she would come find him in the pub. The mystery lady seemed to have no problems seeing right through him and giving as good as she got. He had really enjoyed their brief exchange. The fact that he had no idea what her name was, or even what she really looked like, only added to the intrigue. Maybe once they officially met, he could convince her to stay at the resort for a few extra days. It would certainly make the days ahead a little more tolerable.

Bohdi and the rest of the community at Talisman were still feeling the impact of Jim Mason's death over a month ago. It had been especially hard for Bohdi, as Jim had been his best friend's dad. When the half-owner of the resort passed away, it left a huge pall over the hill. His partner, Cal Stenson, had been hoping to sell the resort to developers for years. It was only Jim's refusal that kept Talisman the gem it was. But with Jim gone, Stenson immediately invited the developers from RG Holdings back to take a look at the place. Rumors were flying that Stenson had managed to convince Jim's daughter Alex to sign off on the sale. She would be arriving later in the week to meet with RG Holdings.

Bohdi shouldn't have been surprised. The last time he had seen little Ally Mason, she had been following her brother Ben and him around. She was like a bad cold that wouldn't go away, spying on them and making sure that all the trouble they found was reported. She had actually been a pretty funny kid, but with six years between her and Ben, she usually fell in the annoying category. After Ben and Ally's parents had divorced, she moved to the city, with only occasional visits back. But after Ben died, Ally never returned.

Jim would tell whoever was listening about his daughter's work as a financial analyst and her successful, busy life in the city.

Too busy to come back for her own father's funeral.

Bohdi wasn't impressed. Funny how she could make it back in order to cash in on the sale of Talisman. Guess everyone has different priorities. It amazed him how people from the same family could turn out so different. Bohdi still held out a small hope that Ally would change her mind and let Talisman remain untouched by cold corporate hands. It was a profitable hill, there was no reason to sell out, unless you count greed. Cal Stenson had been trying to convince Bohdi of the increased returns for the T-Bar if RG Holdings took over the resort. But money wasn't why Bohdi had returned to Talisman and opened his place. He wanted to be surrounded by good snow and good people. He had grown tired of the race. Bohdi still had a few tricks up his sleeve. He wasn't going to watch the warm community atmosphere disappear without a fight.

He had a few days before Jim's daughter arrived. Convincing Cal Stenson was a lost cause, but Bohdi still had a shot. He was going to convince Ally Mason that Talisman was more than an asset to be sold, that it was an amazing community even without revitalization. Hopefully she would see past her own cold, selfish desire, and really see Talisman for the gem it was. He planned on killing her plans with kindness.

But until the prodigal child actually returned, Bohdi was going to spend his time in search of the fascinating woman on the road and getting much further acquainted.

CHAPTER TWO

Alex's breath caught as her father's chalet came in to view. She had forgotten how impressive it was. Designed by an award-winning architect, the combination of nature and luxury had been perfectly realized. Every eye-catching detail was in harmony with the surrounding environment. She had never given much thought to its grandeur while growing up. It was her normal. She realized in this moment it was anything but. Alex was surprised at how skewed her childhood memory had been.

Beautiful high-arched windows and custom masonry that encompassed the base were met by enormous timber pillars that held up a terrace wrapping around to provide a sweeping180-degree view of the valley below. Her father had it built to reflect the magnificence of the towering peaks of mountain above. Alex could feel his presence everywhere.

In the small coupe, crawling up the driveway, Alex gave silent thanks to whichever member of the staff had made sure the drive to her father's chalet was cleared of snow. She doubted she would have the good fortune to be pulled out twice by her mysterious hero. That was probably a good thing. The next time she bumped into him, Alex planned on looking a little more put together. Lipstick probably wouldn't hurt.

It was eerily quiet inside, but from the dark walnut floors that ran throughout, a hint of Old Spice lingered. It was an unexpected reminder of her father. Alex had endeavoured for years to get him to try something new, to no avail. If Jim Mason was one thing, it was resistant to change. She inhaled deeply, thankful now, for that streak of stubbornness.

Looking around, very little had changed. The chalet contained the highest standard of modern conveniences, yet still carried a welcoming rustic charm. The russet leather couch she would curl into with a blanket at the end of the day was still soft to the touch. Alex couldn't remember a time when the stone-clad fireplace that dominated the living room wasn't roaring with the pop and crackle of dry logs. The empty silence spoke volumes to Alex's heavy heart. Turning up the thermostat, she went to drop her bags into her room.

'Oh, Dad.' Alex didn't know whether to laugh or cry. It was exactly the same as the day she had left it, although Alex doubted she had been the one to make the bed. Posters of bands long broken up and medals from her days on the junior ski race team peppered the walls. She opened the drawer of her dresser, stiff from lack of use. There were pictures tucked away beneath an old sweater.

Her chest tightened as she thumbed through the memories. Her family complete, her brother Ben's cocky lopsided grin leaping from the print. She had forgotten how much Ben looked like their dad. Her father had aged so much since Ben's death that it was strange to see his carefree smile in the photo she held. Tears threatened, but Alex tamped them down. They wouldn't change anything, so there was no point in letting the waves of grief pull her in.

She was placing the photos back when something caught her eye. A Polaroid stuck between some papers. Alex pulled out the picture. Her fingers stiffened on the photo. Bohdi Vonn. Smiling, no, he had been laughing. Alex had taken the picture in secret. Bohdi and Ben had been out by the creek, plotting trouble no doubt, she couldn't remember now. What a look he had, all the arrogance of youth. Alex was about to toss out the photo, when she saw something written on the back.

'Alexandra Vonn.' 'Ally Vonn.' 'Mrs. Bodhi Vonn.'

Alex scoffed at her foolish 13-year-old heart. Her all-consuming love – no, obsession – with her brother's best friend had begun the first time Bohdi had come over. That day, at only eight years old, Alex knew exactly whom she was going to spend the rest of her life with. Ben and Bohdi were both 14, which put Alex firmly in 'get lost' territory. She was undeterred and for the next five years, Alex followed them almost everywhere.

But that was a lifetime ago. Alex snapped out of that infatuation when Ben died. She left a lot of childish things behind that day. Love, inhibition, and permanence were only a few. There were times in the years following that Alex had thought about Bohdi, but her mother often reminded her of his reckless behaviour and Alex moved on. Alex threw the photo into the empty wastebasket, along with the memories it held.

Alex rubbed her fingers together, hoping the heat was going to kick in soon. She chided herself for being too lazy to start a fire; instead she decided to find a drink. The kitchen was still fully stocked, at least the bar was. It was obvious that someone had been caring for the place since her father's death. Alex assumed it was Cal Stenson she had to thank. Her father's business partner had never been one to shy away from a glass. It was one of the concerns her father had shared with her during their dinners over the years. Right now, Alex was happy the house was ready for her.

Alex needed to send Cal a text. She was a few days early and wanted to let him know she had arrived. If she gave him a heads up, he could have the resort's books ready and available for her tomorrow. Alex wanted to get a start on the financials. She needed to know exactly what state things were in when she began negotiations with the developers. RG Holdings was a large company with extensive holdings and Alex wanted to be on her A game when they arrived.

Grabbing her phone to call, Alex realized that, although her father had been savvy enough to have Wi-Fi installed, she had absolutely no idea what his password would be. Multiple attempts later, Alex threw down the phone and poured herself a glass of chardonnay.

Standing before the dramatic floor-to-ceiling windows, Alex admired the bustle of the resort community below. The lifts were closing, and she watched as the skiers and snowboarders came whipping down, squeezing in the last runs of the day. Her father's vision of a boutique resort that catered to the discerning ski traveler had truly been realized. The small hotel was nestled between several private villas, all with the same traditional alpine charm. Even the staff accommodations were world class. Her father had convinced a reluctant Cal to restrict any additional dwellings, to preserve the cachet of a chic retreat in the mountains. It was a brilliant move. Her father had been delighted when Talisman was crowned the 'Best Ski Resort' at the World Ski Awards. Taking in the sweeping panorama, Alex could understand why her father had not wanted to leave the snow-covered jewel he had created. It was beautiful, but since Ben's death, she had just not felt the same. Although looking out, in this moment, at the breathtaking view, Alex could not remember why.

So much looked familiar, yet there were small differences too. Alex knew that several additional runs had been opened on the hill over the years, but the biggest change, and the one that caught her interest, was the multileveled stone and wood building at the base of the mountain, opposite to the helipad. There wasn't a flashing neon sign, but the busy crowd indicated that Alex was staring at the T-Bar Pub. To give her stranger credit, it did look like the most fun for miles around. She had no doubt that the atmosphere would be lively with the après ski crowd pouring in.

Alex looked down at the glass in her hand. She was not interested in the end-of-day celebrations, but perhaps after a warm bath and a chance to freshen up, she would be ready to meet her mystery man. Sitting here alone, surrounded by memories, simply did not hold the same appeal as those riveting blue eyes.

***

The bar was packed when Bohdi and Chewie returned. He had left Jaz and Mick in charge while he was in town. With those two crazy Kiwis, he was never sure if the place would still be standing when he got back.

'Haven't burned it down yet, I see!'

Bohdi slid the extra box of glasses he had picked up across the bar towards Mick.

'You're a man of little faith, Bohdi,' Mick clutched his hand to chest. 'Place is chocka today!'

'It's busy every day, Mick. It's how I can afford to keep the high-priced help around,' responded Bohdi.

He was actually really grateful for the bartender and his sister Jaz. They took the majority of work off his hands. In a place like Talisman there was a waitlist of potential employees. Finding quality help was another story. They came from all over the world, fresh from school, or avoiding it, to work for a season or two. The goal was to get as much time on the hill as they could, then head back home, often to wealthy parents, convinced their offspring had learned the value of hard work. They could be a huge pain, but Bohdi understood. It was a fun lifestyle for the young. If it hadn't been for his single-minded obsession with making it to the

Olympics, Bohdi probably would have followed the same path.

'Where's Jaz?'

'Not sure, haven't seen her for a few. She may be outside. Those heaters have been giving us heaps of trouble. May want to have a look.' Mick gave a shrug then turned to a waiting customer.

Bohdi was glad the temperature was supposed to get significantly warmer overnight. When the winds were this cold, the guests preferred room service in the cozy comfort of their hotel rooms. The silent auction was here tomorrow night and he needed the T-Bar full of generous chequebooks if the event was going to be a success.

'Thanks, Mick! If you see her before I do, let her know I need to talk to her.'

'No worries.' Mick nodded, then went back to chatting up the cute brunette whose drink he was taking his sweet time pouring. Bohdi chuckled, shaking his head at the young man's antics.

Bohdi made his way through the throng of people, stopping to chat here and there with the folks who recognized him. He smiled for the camera and freely took selfies with fans, as he kept one eye out for Jaz. He needed to speak with her about the benefit they were having at the T-Bar tomorrow night. He wanted to make sure everything was ready to go, and that they had what was needed. It wasn't really a lot of work; Bohdi just didn't want to be caught up in any last-minute problems if a certain hazel-eyed tourist happened to walk through the door. She hadn't come by yet, but that didn't mean she wouldn't.

'Bohdi!'

Jaz's voice cut through the crowd, a talent that was helpful more often than not. She was a tiny thing, but a force to be reckoned with on a snowboard and a beast on the half-pipe. Bohdi was relieved when she had given up her hero worship and viewed him in a more brotherly fashion. Perseverance was something Jaz had in spades.

Bodhi excused himself from the group he had been talking to and walked to meet Jaz at the door to the patio.

'Problems with the heaters?' asked Bohdi.

'She'll be right. I threatened to use the sledgehammer if they didn't get sorted, and ta da! Working.' Jaz seemed quite proud of herself and Bohdi wasn't going to argue with her methods.

'Great, I just wanted to make sure that things were in order for tomorrow. I think I've got it all prepared and ready to go.'

'So far. Nothing we can't fix in a jiff, if not…' Jaz shrugged. 'Are you ready to be sold off?'

'It's all for a good cause. Anyway, I want it to run smoothly, no surprises, I may have some comp—never mind, I just want to be sure we are good to go.'

Bohdi hoped that he hadn't let too much slip, but Jaz was already squinting at him with pursed lips.

'Don't make me suss it out of you. What gives?'

Inwardly Bohdi groaned. He should have just trusted things would be fine.

'I was hoping for some free time before things got busy, that's all, nothing for you to worry about. You've got enough to do.'

Bohdi hoped that would be the end of it. Jaz could be like a dog with a juicy bone if the mood took.

'I'm female, Bohdi, I know you've never noticed, but we multi-task. So, let's hear it.'

Bohdi sighed. He may as well tell her. Who knows, she might prove helpful.

'Alright, fine,' he conceded. 'I met someone and I'm hoping she shows up here. And if she does, I want to make sure I have a little time.'

‘Well, that’s grand, Bohdi! Don’t know why you didn’t just say so. What’s her name?’

Bohdi had Jaz’s full interest now. She pulled up a stool and sat down, settling in for 20 questions.

‘Uh, I’m not actually sure what her name is. I forgot to ask.’

‘Okay, what does she look like? Are we talking heiress seeks adventure or snow bunny lures in celebrity Olympian?’ Jaz lifted her brow, patiently awaiting a response.

Bohdi accepted the subtle insult of his dating pool. He wasn’t going to deny it was well deserved. There hadn’t been anyone in his life that had been more than a distraction. If any of them had wanted something more, it was often for his celebrity and not his heart. It wouldn’t have mattered anyway… Bohdi wasn’t sure he could share something that still felt broken after all these years.

‘Jaz, the details aren’t important. In fact, I think it’s a little offensive that you’re even asking. Appearances aren’t everything. Anyway, all I’m saying is that I met someone, and I was hoping to get to know her a little better. Not a big deal.’

Bohdi wasn’t about to tell this menace from New Zealand that he actually had no idea who the woman really was. The anonymity of their meeting was now starting to seem less intriguing and more foolish. Why hadn’t he asked her name? Other than eyes that swirled with flecks of green, gold, and mischief, what did he even know of this mystery woman? Jaz was not going to let this go.

‘Ha!’ Jaz thrust a finger into his chest. ‘You don’t even know what she looks like, do you? Is this some internet thi––’

‘No, it is not some internet thing. I met her on the road. Her car was in the bank and I pulled her out. She’s a guest, so I'm hoping she comes through here. That's it. Not a big deal, Jaz.'

Laughing, Jaz slid off the stool and started to walk away. 'You're not acting like it's no big deal, I'm just saying. Maybe she will bid to win the heli-ski trip with you at the auction. I wonder what you're worth?' She wiggled her fingers at him. 'Oooh, romance and mystery are in the air. Will Bohdi Vonn ever meet his elusive love? Stay tuned.'

'You're obnoxious!' Bodhi shouted at the retreating figure.

'You're in trouble!' Jaz hollered back, disappearing into the crowd.

Jaz was probably right. Bohdi was walking around obsessing about a masked woman, a literal masked woman. Imagine when they finally met face to face. There were only two ways this could go. One, she was amazing and they would have a great time together, until she left to go back to a life that didn't include him. This was the most likely scenario, and Bohdi was already starting to feel a little bereft at the thought. Option two was that she would never show. That one was unacceptable now that he had a taste of her quick tongue. He would search this whole mountain to uncover her true identity.

Yeah, Jaz was definitely right. Bohdi couldn't recall a time he had bothered to pursue a woman, and strangely this felt more like a need and not a want. So, for now he would go and help Mick at the bar, making sure that Lothario was actually charging the ladies for their drinks, and prevent himself from spending the whole night watching the front door.

***

Alex gave one last look in the rear-view, patting down a few wayward hairs. Normally she would have been embarrassed to drive such a short distance, but she was hoping to make a better impression this time around and that certainly didn't include static hat head. All her gear was in the car for the walk back; she could stretch her legs later.

A warm bath, a fresh face, and a pep talk in the mirror had gotten her this far; she only needed to step out of this ridiculous car. She gripped the handle, let it go, gripped it again.

'Come on, coward,' she breathed.

It wasn't that difficult. Open the door, close the door, open another door, and find those killer blue eyes and match them to a face. Simple. Alex inhaled and stepped out of the car. The cold encouraged a brisk walk, and she soon faced the beautifully carved wooden doors of the pub. Her mystery man certainly hadn't skimped on the details. The pub was gorgeous from the outside. It complemented the design of the other buildings around the resort. Alex imagined her father had loved the addition. It was strange that he had never mentioned it to her, but then again there was probably a lot he hadn't shared. Alex never made it easy for him when it came to Talisman. His dream was her heartbreak. Some topics weren't discussed. Alex pushed aside the guilt that was edging in. With her father gone, she was realizing that perhaps she could have been less stubborn. She shook her head to brush away the thought. How long was she going to ruminate before she went in? Alex smoothed her jacket and pulled open the door.

Alex shook off the cold, letting the warm air envelop her as she casually scanned the room. The décor was elegant, yet still inviting. She wondered if her father had a hand in its design. Alex made her way to the back and slid onto an empty stool.

'How are ya?'

Alex looked over to see dark chocolate eyes and an open smile. Nope, not her guy. This one was about 10 years too young, but his accent was pretty cute.

'Good, you?' she smiled.

'Sweet as, sweet as.' The young bartender jabbed a thumb over his shoulder. 'What'll you have?'

Alex surveyed her options. She knew if she didn't order something the odds were she would bolt before her mystery man showed. She needed a drink that she couldn't throw back in panic. Nothing that went down too easy.

This level of spontaneity was far from the careful, planned life Alex usually lived. After being convinced by a few work friends that the accuracy of online dating compatibility algorithms would at least provide a probable connection, she agreed to go on a few blind dates. Pleasant enough, but Alex was busy. Romance and love were complicated and certainly never permanent. Alex didn't have the time. What was it about Mr. Blue Eyes that changed that opinion? Alex decided to justify her impulsive behavior by the need for distraction.

'I'll have a scotch on the rocks,' she said. 'With ice. Please.'

The bartender gave her a puzzled look but grabbed a bottle. 'I take it you're not much of a scotch drinker?'

'Is it that obvious?' One smell years ago had been enough to put her off for good.

'Nah, but I'll let you in on a little secret, between you and me.' He leaned in. 'The ice is the rocks.'

Alex's cheeks flamed. 'That's embarrassing.'

'That's alright, barkeeps tell no tales,' he said and he gave her a wink.

'Thank you,' said Alex. The bartender nodded and moved away.

Alex could feel the energy of the pub. Most of the après ski crowd had dispersed, but it was still full. There was no sign of the blue-eyed owner of the T-Bar, but Alex remained hopeful he would show. She waited until the friendly bartender had a free moment.

'Great place.'

'Yeah, heaps of fun. Always something happening. Name's Mick.' He saluted.

Alex tilted her glass. 'I'm Alex. You're from New Zealand?'

His brown eyes opened wide and he nodded. 'Yeah, I'm impressed. Most people go straight to Aussie.'

Alex gave a small laugh. 'I needed to redeem myself to you. Truth is my company had clients from Auckland. You quickly learn the difference if you want to keep the contract.'

'Ha! True.' Mick began to pull beer for a server's tray. 'You ski or board? Or more of a spa and feet by the fire girl?'

'I ski,' replied Alex. 'Wait, feet by the fire? Is that a thing?'

'Could be,' he offered.

Alex could see where a young girl could find herself pulled in by the boy's easy charm. He must have been taking lessons from his boss. Where was his boss?

Mick stumbled behind the bar, nearly dropping the glass in his hand. He glared down at his feet.

'Chewie! Outta the way! You know you're not supposed to be in here.'

Mick nudged the tail end of the golden retriever and looked over apologetically to Alex. 'I love the bag of fur, don't think I don't, he just has—'

'No personal boundaries? So, I've heard.'

'You've met Chewie then? Then I guess that means you've met the boss man too.'

Alex could feel the heat rise to her cheeks once again. 'I have, just haven't seen him… Tonight, I mean.' She was starting to feel foolish. What had she been thinking? Alex glanced at the drink in her hand, grimacing. It was a good thing she had ordered the scotch.

'He's around. Probably found a spot to keep watch on the big door, he's been…Wait!'

'What?' asked Alex.

'You haven't seen him. You! You're the one he pulled out today, yeah?

'Yes, but—'

'Then yup. He's been waiting for you. His eyes have been burning a hole through that door all night. Not sure how he missed you.'

Mick began to look over the crowd, and Alex closed her eyes. Coming here was a foolish miscalculation. What had she been expecting? Eyes meeting across a crowded room? The slow sexy spin of a barstool that left her drowning in pools of sapphire? At least Alex could comfort herself with the knowledge that he had also been eager to see her again. That certainly made a girl feel good.

'It's okay, Mick, I can—'

'No, no. I'll get Jaz to flag down Bohdi for you.'

Alex froze, and her grip tightened on the untouched drink. 'Bohdi?'

CHAPTER THREE

Alex nearly choked as she said it again. 'Bohdi Vonn?'

'Yeah, Olympian, funny, nice guy, all that. You'll love him, everyone does.' Mick gave her a big grin.

Not everyone.

Bohdi Vonn. He was her mystery man, her charming saviour on the road? This could not be happening. Wasn't Bohdi supposed to be off somewhere gathering medals and selling his perfect smile? It was clear now why her father had never mentioned the addition of the T-Bar to her. Bohdi Vonn was a forbidden subject; her father knew how she and her mother felt. Alex never should have come back to Talisman.

Alex could feel her heart beating wildly against her chest. She needed to get out of this place, immediately. She had no desire to bump into Bohdi, now, after successfully avoiding him for 16 years. He may have helped her out today and she appreciated the aid, but one good roadside deed does not erase all memory of the past. She stood up to leave, placing her money on the bar.

'Thanks, Mick—'

Mick reached across the bar to grab her hand. 'No, wait! I can see him, and Jaz will kill me if I let you go! Bohdi! Here!' The determined bartender shouted over the floor and pointed downward in her direction. 'I found her!'

Alex pulled her hand free and ducked down, making a beeline for the door.

'Oomph.'

She ran straight into a wall, a wall of hard flesh and a hint of cedar wood soap. Strong hands steadied her, and Alex looked up into eyes of the purest blue. Bohdi Vonn. She froze. How could she not have remembered those eyes? Sixteen years of purposeful forgetting is how. She had wiped every gorgeous line of his face from memory. Until now.

'Hi! I'm so glad you…' his smile wavered. 'Ally? Little Ally Mason?'

He let go. Her arms suddenly cooled with the loss of his touch.

'It's Alex now. Hello, Bohdi.'

Alex stepped back, straightening her shoulders. She did not want to be any closer to this man than necessary. His presence was already sucking the air from the room. She tried to slow her breath. It was difficult to do when those eyes were looking her up and down. How dare he? She had nothing to prove, certainly not to him.

'It's been a long time, Ally—' He held up a hand. 'Sorry. Alex.'

Alex didn't feel the need to address how much time had gone by. Standing here, in front of Bohdi, it was as if no time had passed at all. Her entire body tingled with nerves and confusion. What on earth was she supposed to say? How was she supposed to react? She was not prepared to come face to face with Bohdi Vonn. Yet here he was. Standing directly in front of her, all six foot three inches of Olympic heartthrob. She needed to stop staring. Alex needed to do what she did best, remove all emotion and control the situation.

'Obviously I had no idea it was you earlier today.'

Bohdi's gaze was intense. 'Obviously,' he replied.

Mick was staring at them in confusion, and with no explanation forthcoming he decided to get back to work and watch them from a safer distance. Alex barely registered Mick's retreat. She was busy applying every yoga trick she knew to control her breathing.

'We heard you would be arriving in a few days. I hadn't expected you so soon.'

How could he sound so casual? Was she the only one affected here? Why didn't he look as stunned as she felt?

'I wasn't aware I was on your schedule.' Alex lifted her chin in defiance.

Bohdi flinched. 'I just meant… I meant I could have welcomed you if I had known. It couldn't have been easy—'

'Welcomed me, to my own home?'

Alex knew she was being churlish, but she couldn't stop. What right did Bohdi have to be standing here, living in the place she had been forced to avoid because of him? Standing here with his ridiculous cheekbones and squared jaw, looking and smelling every bit as good as she remembered.

Alex didn't want to forgive him for his role in her brother's death. Ben would be here now if it weren't for Bohdi. So why wasn't she focused on that anger, the anger she had used all these years to distract her from the pain of grief? She had not forgiven him! Yet here she stood, looking into a face she once worshipped, hating it, while her traitorous heart did flip-flops in her chest. Damn him!

'You haven't been here since—'

'I know how long it's been.'

Bohdi sighed. 'I wasn't trying to be rude, Alex.' He pointed to a quiet table, off to the side. 'Maybe we should talk. It has been a while.'

Alex wished he would stop speaking. The reasonable low baritone of his voice was not helping. Being back at Talisman was difficult enough. She had come to the T-Bar in hopes of pleasant conversation and distraction. That had been a mistake. She didn't need any further reminders of the past. She was going to be surrounded by memories for the next week.

'I need to go, Bohdi, I'm exhausted,' she hesitated. 'But thank you for your help today, I do appreciate it.'

Alex turned to leave, when Bohdi hesitantly touched her shoulder.

'Then let me walk you back. Let it be my final act of charity for the day.' He removed his hand and raised a hopeful brow.

'If you're worried about my safety, I'll be fine,' Alex reassured him.

'Your safety? Please. Little Ally Mason is back on the mountain. It's not you I'm worried about.' The teasing tone that had won her over on the road earlier was back.

'Real nice.' Alex gave Bohdi her best withering stare. She hoped he didn't see the small part of her that was pleased he remembered she had never been a pushover. A very small part.

'Let me walk you.'

'I drove.'

'From Jim's? Your dad's place, I mean?' He didn't smile but those creases were forming next to his twinkling eyes. 'Too far for you to walk these days?'

'I know it's not far; I didn't want my hair… oh, never mind why I drove. I just did.' Alex sighed. 'Listen, Bohdi, it's been a long day with more than a few surprises. I want to go home.'

She shook the keys at him, hoping to make her point. Instead, Bohdi grabbed them and then his jacket as he headed to the door.

'Then I don't know why you are making this so difficult.'

Alex growled at his back and followed him out. It was useless to argue at this point. A few minutes and she would be home and out of the overpowering presence of Bohdi

Vonn. She watched as Bohdi had to fold his long, muscled legs into the driver's seat. Even sliding it back, it was still a tight fit. It was the first time today Alex was pleased she had been given the little coupe. She couldn't stop her corners of her mouth from lifting a little. Bohdi caught her amusement and was undeterred.

'Perfect fit!' he grinned and started the car.

Alex didn't speak as they drove back to the chalet. She didn't need to give him any more opportunities to ooze charm. She was not going to change her mind about him. Not after all these years. She had grown up. A pretty face and a perfect smile didn't alter the facts. They pulled into the drive and up to the garage door.

Bohdi twisted himself out of the car. 'See? No problem.'

Alex shook her head, 'Right. Good night, Bohdi… wait, where are your hat and mitts?'

Bohdi began an exaggerated search of his head.

'Oh no! You'll have to drive me back!'

'Are you—'

'I'm good! I'm good.'

Laughing, Bohdi pulled the items from his coat and punched in the code on the keypad to the garage, handing Alex the keys. She took them but pointed at the keypad.

'How did—'

'Don't worry, there's an extra clicker in the drawer to the left of the fridge.'

Alex was momentarily speechless. 'How would you know? Wait, how often were you here?'

'Enough to know where the extra remote is,' Bohdi replied.

Alex wasn't sure what that meant, but his words stung, reminding her of how little she knew of her father's more recent years here. It was embarrassing that Bohdi was more familiar with her father's home than she was. It was also irritating. It galled her to ask, but Bohdi was likely her best shot.

'You don't happen to know the Wi-Fi password, do you?'

'I do.' He smiled, his face lacking any guile.

Silence. Alex wished she could punch him. Right in his big broad chest, but since she didn't want any further physical contact with him, she was going to have to imagine it. It was much less satisfying than the real thing.

'May I have it?'

'Hmmm… I'm not sure you should. Didn't you tell me you were here for a little rest and relaxation? Maybe some time in the sea salt caves…'

'I never said that, you did. May I have the password… please?' she said, her teeth grinding as she asked.

'I guess I really am playing the part of white knight today,' mused Bohdi.

'Bohdi…' Alex growled his name.

Hand up, Bohdi capitulated. 'Okay, okay. You win. Ignore the beauty around you. Work away.'

'I'm well aware of the beauty around me, thank you,' Alex defended.

'Oh, I don't think you are, Alex.' Bohdi's tone was momentarily serious.

Alex was not getting into this conversation, not tonight, hopefully never.

'Whatever. Password?' she asked.

'Ready?' He paused. 'It's easy to remember.'

Alex pulled out her phone and looked up expectantly. Bohdi put on his mitts and hat. Alex was confused.

'Wait, what? It's easy to remember. That's the actual password?'

Bohdi started laughing. 'Of course not, that would be way too easy to hack. 'Bohdi Vonn is 100% sexy.' That's the actual password. The truth is always easy to remember.'

He flashed another perfect smile. Alex almost threw her phone at him. Bohdi was lucky he didn't lose one of those straight white teeth. He was absolutely maddening.

'That's ridiculous. No, you're ridiculous. My father would never come up with that.'

'You're right, but since I'm the one who set it up…' he shrugged.

'I'm not typing that in.'

Backwards, Bohdi started to walk away from her, down the drive. 'Suit yourself. But remember.' Bohdi cupped his hands together. 'Bohdi Vonn is 100% sexy.'

His voice rang out into the night.

'You're a child!' accused Alex.

Bohdi laughed and turned down the driveway, the back of his hand raised in a wave.

'Goodnight, Ally Mason!'

'It's Alex!' she shouted, but Bohdi didn't seem to hear her.

***

Head upon his pillow, Bohdi stared at the rough-hewn timbers of his ceiling.

He never considered a third option, certainly not one in the form of Ally Mason. No, Alex. He would do well to remember that, lest she be tempted to slug him. Bohdi had the feeling only her immense control had prevented that tonight. He didn't know why he felt the need to bait her so much.

She had caught him completely off guard. It was hard to believe that wild, ponytailed child had turned into such a stunning woman. Then again, maybe it wasn't so shocking. Ben Mason had been a golden boy too.

Bohdi was still trying to reconcile the fact that the mysterious and flirtatious woman on the road was Alex Mason. His damsel in distress had been quick with a retort, but it was still light, still pleasant. Her uncovering of his identity had given Alex a much sharper edge. Bohdi wasn't sure what to think. There were too many questions. Which one was the real Alex Mason? Why the immediate animosity? How much influence had her mother had? He hadn't seen Alex since she and her mother left after Ben's accident. He could understand how seeing him could be a painful reminder of her brother. Had her father not mentioned the T-Bar or Bohdi to her?

Now Bohdi had a bigger problem on his hands. He had thought his nemesis would be a cold, selfish woman intent on selling his mountain to the highest bidder. He wasn't expecting a quick-witted beauty whose heart may still be aching alongside his own.

He was going to have to take a whole new approach. Alex was angry – Bohdi wasn't a fool – but he also wasn't mistaken about the connection he had felt on that road. He was sure Alex had felt it too, otherwise why had she come to the T-Bar? He was going to have to find a way to persuade Alex that both the mountain and the man deserved a chance.

'What do you think, buddy?'

Chewie rolled over and flopped on Bohdi's legs. Bohdi rubbed a silky ear.

'Yeah, me too. Get some rest, boy. I think we are going to have our work cut out for us.'

CHAPTER FOUR

The early morning sun peeked through the blinds of the great window, sending broken beams of light across the bed. Alex cracked one eye open, groaning at the interruption to her sleep. She had planned on taking advantage of her work sabbatical to sneak a few extra hours of sleep in the morning. After tossing and turning all night, trying to shake the vision of teasing blue eyes, she was exhausted. Bohdi Vonn. It was bad enough he was trying to thwart her sale of Talisman to RG Holdings. Did he need to steal her sleep too?

Rolling over in the king-sized bed, Alex pulled the pillow tightly over her head; she could block out the light, but it was a lot harder to block out reality.

'Ughh…' she moaned.

Sitting up, Alex looked across the bed to the mirror on the wall. She was a mess. She ran a hand down her hair, hoping to bring some dignity back to her reflection. Her fingers caught on the snarled hair at the back of her head. More evidence of her restless night, and another grievance to place at Bohdi's feet.

'Ughh…' Alex flopped back to the pillows.

Alex could only imagine if her mother could see her now. Elizabeth Mason was an expert at silent disapproval. Alex had never seen her with a hair out of place. She was certain that if one dared, a single withering glare would immediately set it to rights. She was always lovely though.

Her mother had not been pleased when Alex decided to return to Talisman to manage the sale to the developers. There were 'people' to handle these things and she couldn't understand why Alex was getting involved. Alex wasn't fooled. Her mother knew exactly why, but Elizabeth Mason could be purposefully obtuse when the situation warranted. Her mother had no desire to return once she had made her grand exit; therefore, Alex should have no reason. After Ben's accident when out with Bohdi, her mother had been devastated and righteous in her fury. She had railed against her ex-husband and demanded that Bohdi's name never be spoken again. Alex understood her mother's pain, but she still needed her father. It was only ever the two of them, Alex and her father, on the occasions he came to the city. Elizabeth Mason had simply moved on, back to her role as the chairman of the Hope Foundation. Hosting galas and soirees, Talisman a distant memory. Alex wondered how her father had handled his wife's departure. He had never spoken a single word against her. If avoidance was hereditary, then Alex had gotten it in spades.

She needed to get up. She also needed to punch in that stupid password Bohdi set up. It galled her to know that he knew she was typing it in. She could hear that laugh. Unfortunately, she needed access to her email and her accounts, and she didn't want to be in the hustle and bustle of the hotel while trying to work. She also didn't want to increase her chances of running into Bohdi. The resort village was such a small place that it was already going to be a challenge avoiding him.

She grabbed her phone. Might as well get it over with.

'Bohdi Vonn is 100% sexy.' Did she really need to say the words aloud as she keyed it in? The arrogant man was right. It was easy to remember. Stupid password.

It had barely been accepted when the notifications started flooding in. There were so many, the phone nearly vibrated out of her hand in its demand for her attention. There were at least a hundred messages. It had been, what, 24 hours, maybe? She put the phone back on the nightstand with a heavy sigh. This is exactly why she needed a change, why she needed to sell this place and move on to the next chapter of her life. She was weary of the game and constantly running on empty. She needed to make this deal happen. Sell Talisman, leave it and the painful memories behind, and get on with living life again. In order to do that she needed to get over to see Cal Stenson.

Alex pulled open the blinds to the ridge above. The sky was a glorious blue and free of clouds. Yesterday's weather had blown right through during the night. While her preference may have been for sand and sun, there was no denying the breathtaking beauty of a bluebird day. Clear skies after a night's snowfall were sure to have the guests in a hurry to be on the hill.

After a quick bite to eat, Alex decided to walk to Cal's office, giving herself some fresh air that would hopefully clear her head. It was crisp, but not truly cold. The perfect conditions allowed a pang of regret that she had not brought her skis. That thought didn't last long, as Alex knew there were far more pressing matters to contend with.

Walking past the first chairlift on the right edge of the mountain, Alex noticed a woman greeting the skiers and boarders as they entered the lines. Each one received a hug.

'Freda!!' Alex called across the path

She couldn't believe it. Freda Bauer! Alex had assumed she would have retired years ago. She must be younger than Alex remembered. Strange the way a child perceives their world. Freda was still giving out hugs to each guest, after all these years. The realization sent warmth straight down to her toes.

'Freda!' Alex shouted again and headed over to the lift. Freda's whole face lit with pleasure as she recognized who had been calling her name.

'Ally! Come! Let me see you.'

Freda clasped her hands together and then grabbed Alex's hands, pulling her in tightly for a hug. Freda was one of those wonderful additions that made Talisman so special. She had seen hardened politicians welcome an embrace from the diminutive Austrian. Alex had been sure as a child that it was Freda's attempt at encouraging world peace. Looked like she had never stopped trying. Freda stepped back to look up at Alex. 'You're as beautiful as your mother, but there is so much of Benny in that face too!'

Holding Alex's hand, Freda moved them away from the crowd.

'I'm so sorry about your father.' Freda squeezed her hand. 'He was such a good man, and so very proud of you. He talked about you all the time.'

'Thank you, Freda.' Alex discreetly moved on from the subject of her family. 'How have you been? I can't tell you how wonderful it is to see you!'

'Come now, I'm getting old, that's how I've been.' Freda gave Alex a nudge. 'And loving every minute of it. Arlo and I should be grandparents soon, and the ski program is running as it should.'

Freda and her husband Arlo looked to be a mismatched pair. He was tall, she was tiny, and while Freda was as light as a feather, Arlo was solid European brawn. Alex loved them both. Her father had invited them over from Austria, after meeting them during après ski in Soll. He wanted to create a world-class ski platform and he found the perfect couple to do it. Alex and Ben had both been in their program, Bohdi too. They had been like a second set of parents. When she was still living out here, she spent more time with Freda than her own mother. It was incredible to think the pair would soon be grandparents.

'Congratulations! That's wonderful. You will both be amazing grandparents.' Alex looked around. 'Where is Arlo? Here at the hill?'

Freda waved her hand about and said, 'Oh, he's here somewhere. I don't bother to keep track. The Little Tigers will be meeting soon. You can probably find him giving sage advice to attentive three-year-olds.'

The little woman was jesting, but Alex had no doubt that the children actually were attentive. When a six foot four, red-bearded giant stands before you, you tend to pay attention. She remembered how she had once believed he looked like he climbed down the mountain one day to join the people below. She imagined he aged well. Arlo commanded attention, but there was no softer soul.

'I will keep an eye out,' Alex promised. 'If I hear the small cries of children, I will know where to look.'

'Have you bumped into Bohdi yet?'

Her question was innocent, but Alex knew how quickly rumours could fly in the village. She really didn't want to discuss Bohdi with Freda, or anyone for that matter.

'I have.' Her reply to Freda was curt, but the woman did not seem to notice.

'Oh wonderful. We had all heard you were coming home—'

'Well, it's not really home anymore, Freda.'

'Of course it is. Don't be silly. This will always be your home.'

'You knew I was coming, so you have heard why I am here.' Alex spoke gently; she didn't want to be rude, but it seemed that no one was accepting the inevitable.

'I've heard lots of things in my time. Some true, some not. I do know that many times things can change. It's no matter. I am pleased you are here.' Freda gave Alex's arm a pat. 'Tell me you are still skiing, yes?'

Alex put up both hands in supplication. 'I wouldn't dare stop,' she laughed. It had been about two years since she had last been on skis, but she would never confess that to her former instructor. Freda was as happy to use her arms to infuse you with love, as her hands to crack the whip.

'Wonderful! You will find time while you are here to ski with Bohdi then? It has been so nice to have him back. Such a time that child has had. It will be good for you both to share time together.'

Such a time? That child? Freda had a kind heart, but that was a little much. There wasn't much to Bohdi's life that appeared overly difficult. The country adored him, and he had been the face of heaven knows how many advertising campaigns. Enough that she was thankful for the advent of the DVR. And what exactly did Freda think they were going to share? Bohdi may still be the picture of perfection, but Alex had grown up, and she did not need to revisit any memories with Bohdi Vonn. If Freda didn't recognize that, Alex wasn't going to explain it. She didn't need Freda to take on her concerns. But right now it was easier to go along. Ahh, classic Mason emotional avoidance, she really was good at it.

'We'll have to see. I'm going to be awfully busy. But you are right, it would be lovely to have a run or two down the hill.'

'Take the time. The world can wait. You don't always have to be running, moving, and working. Enjoy the moment. You'll remember that when you get to the top of Haig Ridge again. I can think of no better view.'

Freda's wistful words struck a chord with Alex. There were times as a child she had felt invincible, standing on the top ridge of Talisman, looking down to the gingerbread village below.

'You're right, Freda, I will find the time.' Alex patted the pocket of her jacket. 'In order to find that time I need to go see Cal. That's where I was headed, before I was sidetracked by the wonderful surprise of you.'

'Charming you are, just like your brother was. That boy could convince me of nearly anything.' Freda didn't wait for her to respond. 'Off you go then, we will chat later. Right now I see some young men who look like they need the arms of a dazzling older woman. I never disappoint.'

Alex fought the urge to laugh aloud. She had almost forgotten how endearing Freda was. She lived with an open heart, not only embracing people, but life too. Alex wished she could find that for herself. Perhaps she would, once this sale went through and she could get on with the rest of her life.

Buoyed by her fortunate run-in with Freda, Alex continued to Cal's office. She needed to get those books from him. She only had a few days before the reps from RG Holdings arrived, and she needed to see what she was dealing with.

The sun had grown brighter and Alex put on her sunglasses, taking a moment to glance at the T-Bar. She would have to walk past it on her way to Cal's. She hoped that luck would be on her side, and there would be no run-in with Bohdi this morning.

***

'Well, Freda got a hug out of her, Chewie. Maybe she will be a little friendlier today with some rest and a little love.' Bohdi looked down at the retriever. 'We can thank Freda later for taking one for the team.'

He watched as Alex and his former instructor spoke on the hill. He would love to overhear their conversation. Was Freda explaining to her that selling Talisman was a horrible idea and a slap in the face to her father's legacy? Alex was still smiling, so he had a feeling that Freda was taking a subtler route. They seemed to be getting along fine.

It could be possible that Alex simply didn't like him. It certainly appeared to be the case. She had been friendly enough – no, more than friendly – when they had first met. But that was before she knew who she was talking to. Bohdi wasn't used to provoking such a reaction from someone. It was bothering him that he couldn't figure out why.

'She liked you alright, boy. Maybe she prefers hairy and cute over ruggedly handsome.'

Chewie was unimpressed by his jest. He jumped up, resting his front paws on the sill of the window that Bohdi was watching from. He gave a soft bark and moved back down. Trotting over to the stairs, he barked again, wagging his tail.

'Not a chance, buddy. She only looks friendly. If you want to go out there, you're on your own.'

Chewie stepped onto the stairs, his tail wagging, banging against the floor. 'Go ahead, but don't come crying back to me when she sends you packing. She's aware we're friends, you know.'

Bohdi turned to look back out the window and heard the quick patter of Chewie's feet as his dog deserted him. 'Figures. Girl comes along and bam, so long guys night.'

He couldn't blame the mutt. Bohdi would have liked to go out and talk to Alex too. He knew the welcome he would receive. He didn't know why he cared so much. Alex Mason had come back to sell Talisman, not make nice with the locals. He needed to remember that she wasn't her father, nor was she her brother. Alex had spent most of her teen years and adult life under the complete tutelage of Elizabeth Mason. Could she even remember the days where fun and laughter were part of the package? Was she upset by the relationship that Bohdi had with Jim?

It had been a natural progression for the two men. A father missing his son and a boy missing his best friend. They had been able to share their grief and pain over the last several years. Jim had tried to help Bohdi overcome his guilt over Ben's death, but that had proven too hard to do.

When Bohdi had finally made the Olympic team, Jim had been there, cheering him on. Every competition, every race, Bohdi fought, not for himself, but for Ben too. He pushed himself to his limits each time, but never could he fully succeed. Silver was easy. Gold always out of reach. When his determination ended with injury and his chances for gold were gone, Bohdi turned to film and stunt work, pushing every limit. He had been working on a film for Warren Miller when Jim had proposed a change. Bohdi had been so tired and was grateful for the opportunity.

Between Jim, Chewie, and the people that held Talisman together, Bohdi finally felt like he could stop running. He had been chasing something he couldn't define, proving something he couldn't name. But then Jim died, and when Bohdi didn't think his heart could break anymore, along came Alex Mason, ready to sell off the one thing that made him feel close to whole.

Bohdi pressed his face to the window. And now it looked like she was taking his dog too.

Alex had stopped on her path to Cal's office to bend down and pet Chewie. The traitorous dog was lapping it up. The old adage about a loyal dog obviously didn't apply to golden retrievers. He should have gotten a border collie. At least they were smart and loyal. He wouldn't have to remind a collie which side his bread was buttered on.

'Oh, I see you, dog. This better be part of an elaborate scheme to save this mountain or you're sleeping on the floor tonight.'

It was under his breath that he muttered the words, but it wouldn't matter even if Chewie could actually hear him. His dog knew Bohdi was a soft touch. One sad whine and the big sack of fur would be off the floor. Besides, Chewie wasn't the problem. The fact that he was peeking through the window of his own home at his beautiful nemesis was an embarrassment. Bohdi needed to get his game back on. There was a time when she thought he walked on water. He needed that girl back. He just wasn't sure if it was to only save his mountain, or because he wanted to remember what it felt like to be loved for more than fame and fortune. He needed to get out from behind the curtains and put all effort into winning back the mountain and the girl.

CHAPTER FIVE

'Alex!' exclaimed Cal, as she entered his office. 'What are you doing here?'

Cal's face pulled into a grimace and his back stiffened against the leather of his chair. Alex stood, rather shocked at his response, her hand still on the edge of the door.

'Wow, that wasn't the welcome I was expecting. Should I come back later?'

Alex motioned out the door with her hand but didn't move. His jaw tightened and forehead creased as he gathered the papers about his desk, quickly piling them together.

'No, no. Sorry, Alex. You caught me off guard. I only meant I wasn't expecting you. Please sit down. Do you need a drink?' Alex could only stare at her father's business partner of the past 20 years. He must have sensed her discomfort.

'Coffee, I mean, coffee, tea—'

'I'm fine, thank you.' Alex needed to cut him off. This whole situation was becoming awkward. 'How have you been? I know it has been a long time since we have seen each other.' She took a deeper look across the desk. Cal really did look rough. He had been a somewhat attractive man once, but the grey of his eyes was lost in the sagging eyelids and dark circles below. He looked exhausted. Alex reminded herself not to judge him too harshly. After all, it had been

Cal who had been singlehandedly running Talisman since her father had passed. She should be thanking him, not giving him the once-over. Cal looked relieved at the change of topic.

'As good as an old man can be these days. Seeing you here reminds me of how old that is.' Cal leaned towards her. 'Again, I want to say in person, I am really sorry about your dad, Alex. It was a shock to us all.'

'Thank you, Cal. It has been strange being back. I do wish I had been here for his service,' she replied.

'I think he was taking his cue from you. He knew—'

She held up her hand. 'It's okay, you've already explained.'

Alex didn't want to rehash her father with Cal. They had already spoken on the phone several times. She wanted to get started on the sale.

'I was hoping to grab Talisman's books from you. I want to run through everything before RG Holdings arrives. Make sure we are in the best shape possible for the sale.'

Cal started to fiddle with the paper pile he had created, while readjusting his weight in his chair.

'The books?' he asked. Wiping his brow, Alex could see little beads of perspiration on his forehead. It was not that hot. Was Cal sick? Is that why he was pushing this sale? She hoped not, but the poor man certainly looked uncomfortable.

'Yes, if you don't mind. I want to be sure I am prepared for any negotiation with the RG reps.'

'Why didn't you call to let me know that you wanted them? Or that you had arrived?'

Alex wasn't sure why Cal still looked rather offended that she hadn't let him know of her arrival. Perhaps she should have called, she had intended to, but her phone didn't have service. She still couldn't see why it was such a big deal.

'I had planned to, but,' Alex waved her phone, before placing it on his desk, 'no service at the chalet. I needed the Wi-Fi password.'

He still didn't look pacified. 'Why wouldn't you use the house phone?'

The phone? Alex felt the tinge of embarrassment on her cheeks. Of course, the phone! Alex had been so long without a landline in the city that she hadn't even thought to look. She was such a fool. Alex was glad that Bohdi hadn't known of her error. His smug satisfaction with her Wi-Fi need was more than enough. She could only imagine if he knew she had completely forgotten the existence of an actual landline phone. He would—wait. Why was she even thinking about Bohdi right now? The man was like an insidious poison infecting her mind. She needed to focus on the task at hand.

'Sorry, Cal. The truth is I completely forgot about the phone,' she shrugged. 'Either way, I am here now. So…'

'I'll grab them,' he said and pushed himself from the desk. The corners of his mouth pulled down, as though he were complying under duress to her request.

'Thank you, Cal. I really do want this sale to go through quickly and smoothly.'

Those words seemed to pick up the man's spirits. He gathered the requested info while he spoke.

'I am so glad to hear you say that. I know we talked on the phone, but this really is the best option for us both. For Talisman too. RG has the resources to really make this place great.'

'It's already pretty great, Cal.' Alex had no idea why she was defending Talisman.

For a moment, Cal looked nervous. 'I only meant, more. They will make it more of the great place it already is.'

'Absolutely,' she reassured. 'I think this is a good idea. You want to move on, and so do I. Change isn't always bad. In fact, change can be really beneficial. Like this sale.'

Cal beamed. 'Exactly! I am so glad you get that. Your mother understood that. Your father, on the other hand… Well, you know how stubborn Jim could be. Like pulling teeth sometimes.'

He was looking over to Alex for her agreement, but Alex only found she was becoming irritated with Cal. She knew exactly how stubborn her father was, and she didn't need anyone else expressing it. The two men had been partners for a long time, but without her father's vision this place wouldn't even exist. Of course, Cal had contributed. There was no way to put together a project like this without a money-man. He had probably gone up against the brick wall of Jim Mason numerous times. She understood that, and she respected that. Alex just didn't want to hear it. Her dad was gone, and Cal was finally getting his way. She wanted to leave it at that.

'Yeah. I think I will grab these and head out, Cal.'

Alex gathered the binders he had put on the desk. She reached into her pocket and then handed him a memory stick. 'Throw the rest of the files on here.'

Cal hesitated as he took the stick. 'I can bring it by later if you like?'

Alex shook her head. 'I'll wait. It should only be a few minutes.'

He plugged it in, and again tried for casual conversation. 'Plan on any skiing while you're here? I'm sure Freda and Arlo would love to see you. Bohdi Vonn is here too. You remember him? Local boy makes good? I'm sure he would be happy to take you out for the day. In fact, why don't I take care of all of this, and you go take a break? You do this all the time… why don't you go enjoy your time here.' He must have realized from her open mouth that she was far from convinced and he continued his attempts. 'It's what your father would have wanted.'

It wasn't often that Alex was at a loss for words, but Cal had managed to throw her off guard. *Do you remember Bohdi Vonn?* Was he kidding? Was she the only one that could remember what happened here? It was as though the universe was planning some awful joke, determined to throw Bohdi on her path at every turn. In order for her to move on and get to that bloody beach she dreamed of, she would have to first overcome the larger-than-life obstacle of Bohdi Vonn.

She was getting tired of hearing his name, especially in connection with hers. Maybe she needed to give her mother a call, in order to get a little perspective again. There must be something in the mountain air that had people breathing the Bohdi Vonn Kool-Aid. Well, Alex wasn't going to stay long enough to get sucked in. Alex ignored the comment completely.

'Yes, I bumped into Freda. It was wonderful to see her.' The screen beeped and Alex removed the stick herself. Holding it up, she said, 'Thanks, Cal.'

She was all done with this conversation today. She was going back to the chalet and she was not going to think about Bohdi Vonn again. Alex put on her sunglasses, grabbed the binders, and headed back outside.

She had barely made it a few feet when Chewie came bounding up to her. Earlier she had seen the affectionate dog, but thankfully not his master. Squinting at the trail between Cal's office and the chalet, she could see she wasn't going to be that lucky again.

'Seriously, Chewie, I'm starting to think I'm cursed,' said Alex.

Up ahead on the patio of the T-Bar was Bohdi. There was another man with him, but he was bent over so she couldn't make him out.

Chewie was winding around her legs, encouraging her to keep moving.

'Fine, I'll walk with you, but I'm not talking with him. There is nothing we have to say to each other.'

Alex could feel her heart starting to beat rapidly as she approached the T-Bar. She must be seriously out of shape, if this short walk had her catching her breath.

'Alex!' Bohdi gave a cheery wave.

Ugh, was he always this friendly? If he could read her thoughts, she doubted he would be. Chewie bounded ahead, sticking his head through Bohdi's legs, demanding a rub. 'I see Chewie has tracked you down.'

The man who had been bending down attempted to stand up, in the process whacking the back of his head on a table.

'Ow!' he grunted and then stood up. 'Ally? Is that really Ally Mason, or have I smacked my head too hard? Am I seeing things?'

'Arlo!' Alex put down the binders, pulled off her glasses, and threw herself into the bearish grip of Freda's husband.

Bohdi cleared his throat, interrupting the reunion. 'A heads up, it's Alex now, Arlo.'

Alex shot Bohdi a dirty look and stuck out her tongue. She quickly regretted it as she watched an amused smile spread across Bohdi's face. What was it about that man that made her act like a spiteful child?

Arlo held her out from him, giving her the once-over.

'*You* can call me Ally, Arlo,' she said.

'Well, I think a grown woman can have a grown-up name. Alex it is,' replied Arlo.

Alex was so pleased to see Arlo, despite the company he was keeping. Bodhi was everywhere she turned. She was starting to wonder if his only protest to RG Holdings purchasing Talisman was that they hadn't agreed to rename it 'Bohdi World.'

'What are you up to?' she asked the giant Austrian.

Once again Bohdi interrupted. 'Fixing the heaters. If Jaz isn't here to glare at them, they fizzle out.'

‘Isn’t there a maintenance crew that can handle that?’

‘Sometimes a man likes to get his hands dirty.’

Arlo weakly stifled a laugh and sat down, content to watch their exchange. He was probably another fan of *The Bohdi Vonn Show*.

‘Well, when you’re done playing, I’m sure we can get an electrician here to sort it out.’

‘I’ve only begun… playing. A man needs to take his time, if he wants things to work out right.’ Bohdi’s smile was as innocent as his words, but wicked lurked behind those blue eyes, and Alex hadn’t missed its flicker.

‘Then a man should focus on the task at hand and keep his mind off distractions.’

‘Some distractions are worth it,’ he countered.

‘I find most distractions are exactly that, a diversion and nothing more. Empty, fleeting, and not worth it in the end. Only takes your eyes off the big prize.’

‘And what is the big prize, Alex Mason, your—’

‘Okay…’ Arlo cut him off, and Alex narrowed her eyes at Bohdi, daring him to continue.

‘How long are you here for, Alex? Will we get a chance to spend some time with you?’ asked Arlo.

Alex tamped down all the clever retorts she had lined up to shoot at Bohdi and with some difficulty turned her attention back to Arlo.

‘Yes, I would love a chance to visit with you and Freda, Arlo.’ Alex emphasized the Austrian couple’s names as she gave a brilliant smile in Bohdi’s direction. ‘I won’t be here long. Once things are wrapped up, I have a date with sun, sand, and the next stage of my life.’

Arlo pointed to the binders on the table. ‘What are you up to?’

‘I’ve grabbed Talisman’s books from Cal—’

‘Anything you need to grab here?’ Bohdi interjected.

Alex ignored him, cleared her throat, and continued speaking. 'I'm going to take a quick peek, see what things look like.'

Arlo nodded his approval. 'Your father was very proud of you. Said that mind of yours worked a mile a minute.' He gave a short laugh. 'No surprise to those of us charged with keeping you reigned in all those years ago. I'm teasing you, Alex, but your father was very proud of your success.'

Alex blushed under both the praise and the reminder of her childhood antics. Sixteen years and it was like she had never been gone a day. One stern look from Arlos's bushy brows and Alex was eight years old again. Despite her mother's protest, their father had let them run wild throughout the resort. There was always a set of eyes to keep a lookout, but those were different times. That freedom had groomed a confidence in both Alex and Ben. Perhaps too much confidence. Ben's death had put an end to Alex's rash behavior. Instead, she channelled that energy into a life of predictable outcomes and measured results. Numbers and methodology, not emotions and unpredictability. Alex hadn't removed all fun, she had simply reduced risk. She felt a small twinge of regret at the loss of childhood freedom, but it was soon quieted. It was a reminder that not all her memories of Talisman were negative, but also that those kinds of antics were not worth the risk. They weren't.

'Thank you, Arlo, and perhaps an apology is long overdue. I may have been a little unruly.' She gave him a smile of chagrin. Arlo waved it away.

'You were all… what did you say? Unruly? That's putting it mildly.' He gave a loud laugh and clapped Bohdi on the shoulder. 'But you were kids.' He shrugged, as if that explained it all.

Chewie had apparently waited long enough for the conversation to end. He began to nose at Alex's pocket, and

Alex reached in to pull out some cheese. She started to unwrap the treat.

'Cheese?' Bohdi seemed stumped. 'You carry cheese in your pocket? No wonder Chewie likes you so much.'

'I thought I might get hungry—'

'And you stuck some cheese in your coat? You are full of surprises.'

'It's what was in the fridge,' defended Alex. She knelt down, breaking the cheese in pieces and popping them in Chewie's mouth. 'You're glad I had some. Right, boy?' She stood and turned back to Bohdi.

'Perhaps I am full of surprises, Bohdi, but you are not. You are exactly the same as you have always been. You haven't changed at all.'

Alex was sure her words had hit their mark, until Bohdi gave her a long, slow head-to-toe inspection. She could feel her skin warm as the heat coming from those eyes hit her. She wanted to put him in his place, but instead she stood there, allowing his gaze to send tingles throughout her whole body.

'I can't say the same, Alexandra. You've changed a whole lot.'

Bohdi drew out her full name, like he was tasting it on his lips. He didn't bother to hide his meaning. Alex saw the same intimate interest in his eyes that she had seen out on the road, when he had pulled her out. She wished she had a clever retort, but her brain was no longer connected to her tongue. She was thinking of all the times she had dreamed of this exact moment as a little girl. When the man she so desperately adored, Bohdi Vonn, finally recognized that she had grown up and wanted her like she wanted him. Only now it came too late. She was not going to be pulled in by his full lips and the thought of them on her skin, his low voice whispering her name, like an offering to the gods of pleasure. No, she would not.

She grabbed the books from the table. 'I need to go.'

Alex stood on the tips of her toes and kissed Arlo's cheek. 'I'm glad I saw you. We will have a better visit soon.'

Arlo was silent, nodding his agreement.

A heavy sigh escaped, as Alex turned and walked toward the chalet, Chewie at her heels.

***

'She doesn't like me, Arlo.'

Bohdi winced as he watched the swaying backside of Alex Mason accompanied by his turncoat mutt. He couldn't stop his imagination from peeling off those layers she had been hiding behind since he found her stuck on the road. Granted, he wasn't trying overly hard. He longed to slide back each one she wore like armour and reveal the real woman beneath. Problem was he didn't see himself getting past the first zipper. Little Miss Numbers would tell him the likelihood was close to zero percent. But a man does not medal at the Olympics if he isn't willing to challenge the odds. Right now they were stacked against him.

He watched as Alex bent down, giving Chewie a final pat, sending his reluctant dog back to the pub. 'I know how you feel, buddy,' he muttered.

It was like some strange twist of the universe. The annoying girl who once followed him relentlessly around the resort no longer had any interest in his company. When did he get drawn in to this ridiculous role reversal? He never pursued anyone. Why was he now trying to find any opportunity to throw himself in her path while Alex was going out of her way to avoid him?

She was still annoying, this time in a very different way. The *can't shake the image of her with her head thrown back and his name on her lips* sorta way. What was he doing? And why wasn't Arlo answering him?

Turning to face his mentor, Bohdi was taken aback by Arlo's blank stare. 'I mean she really doesn't like me, Arlo.'

The large Austrian looked over his shoulder at Alex's retreat then returned his gaze to Bohdi. 'Can you blame her?' he asked.

His words took Bohdi by surprise. He shook his head at Arlo. 'What do you mean? I was perfectly—'

'Obnoxious,' Arlo finished for him. 'Absolutely, utterly, completely obnoxious. Am I being too subtle? Wait, you can't answer that, as you've clearly shown me you have no idea what that word means.'

Bohdi's eyes widened and his jaw dropped. That wasn't fair. Arlo was way off on this one. 'Well, I don't know if obno—'

'I do, because I was standing here. Listening to it.' Arlo's bushy brows lowered, nearly obscuring his glaring eyes. 'Let me tell you something, Bohdi. You see that sweet tiny thing over at the lift, the one handing out hugs like they were candy?'

Arlo pointed over in Freda's direction. Bohdi was wise enough to just nod. He had been on the receiving end of Arlo's famous lectures on more than one occasion.

'That itty bitty woman would have cut out my heart, fed it to me, and insisted that I thank her for supper if I ever spoke to her the way you spoke to that girl.'

'Well, she's not really a girl anymore, Arlo. She's more–
–'

Arlo held up a hand. 'Quiet. I think you've talked enough. I don't know what has gotten into you today, but you need to shake it off. I know you're worried about what she is going to do now that Jim is gone. But if this is your plan to help that, you'd better rethink your strategy.'

Chastised, Bohdi was suitably chagrined. 'I don't know, Arlo. I guess I'm not used to having someone dislike me quite so intensely.' He quickly continued before Arlo once again reminded him of his poor behavior. 'To be fair, she wasn't pleased to see me before I even said a word.'

'Fair enough,' Arlo conceded. 'That was the coldest reception I've seen you receive in quite some time.' The old man laughed. 'Maybe she is the right balance for that ego of yours.'

'My ego?' Bohdi attempted to look wounded by the man's words.

Arlo shrugged. 'At least she likes Chewie.' Arlo started to walk away. 'I'm heading over to the school. There's a fresh pack of kids for me to share all this wisdom with. Maybe one of them will actually listen.'

Bohdi watched the big man lumber off. Arlo was right. Bohdi couldn't resist needling Alex. He had no idea what was wrong with him. That was a lie. He knew what was wrong. It was every shade of blonde you could imagine twisted into the prettiest braid of sunshine and honey that came to rest beside a long, smooth neck. It was hazel-colored eyes that had shot laughter, irritation, and sadness in his direction in less than 24 hours. It was perfect bow-shaped lips that shared an open smile with his friends and thinned when focused on him. It was legs, well, he actually had no idea what her legs looked like, but his mind could fill in the blanks. It was all those things. Those absolutely ridiculous things. What a switch this turned out to be. Alex would probably laugh if she knew.

Bohdi wished he could push these thoughts from his mind. He was practically swooning over a woman who clearly felt nothing for him at all. He was used to being fawned over, not the other way around. He liked it that way. Never too attached, always keeping it light. He never wanted to be in a relationship where someone became too dependent on him. He didn't want to be in the position where he could let someone he cared about down. He never wanted to fail to protect again.

So, what could possibly draw him to the one person who planned to do away with the only thing he cared most about? Why was he letting his mind wander to places he had long since locked away? What was his plan? Fall in love with Ben's little sister? Convince her that he could be more than a brief resort fling? It would be a lie. Even if he wanted more, Bohdi knew he could never be the one for Alex. He didn't measure up. She deserved someone she could count on, who could always keep her safe. He couldn't offer her more because he didn't have it to give. He needed to accept that now, before things got out of his control.

CHAPTER SIX

Nestled into her corner of the couch, Alex slid the memory stick into her laptop. Memory stick. If only real memories were dealt with so easily. Pick and choose the files you wished to remember. Or even the ability to hide the files you didn't wish to see. Like the barest hint of dimples that brought a strong, chiselled jawline from Neanderthal into heartthrob territory. How one incisor was almost threatening rebellion from its straight pearly companions, but never did turn. Or that wonderfully mischievous smile that once turned on you, sent tingles throughout your whole body, leaving you defenseless from the onslaught of brilliance. Like eyes so blue they made a cloudless sky appear as though it was barely putting in effort.

The problem was that she couldn't erase any of them, and certainly not the big flagged file of her brother's death. So now, instead of working, doing what she had come to Talisman to do, she was sitting back on the same couch she sat on years ago, thinking about the same boy.

To be fair, it wasn't completely her fault. Everywhere she turned, someone was talking about Bohdi, or she was bumping into the man himself. It was like he had completely taken over her resort. Her resort? Yes, for a few more weeks at least, it was hers. Not Bohdi's. Unless he planned on purchasing Talisman outright, she didn't care how much money he had, or how famous he was, he still had no right to look so comfortable on her land and especially in her house.

That was a whole other irritation. How much time had Bohdi and her father spent together? His intimate knowledge of her drawers was not only smug, but annoying. Why had he been spending so much time here? Was he trying to replace the son her father had lost? Or was he trying to usurp her position as his remaining child?

Pangs of guilt reminded Alex that she had been the one who controlled the direction of her relationship with her father. He had always taken her lead. And although she knew the truth of the matter, she much preferred to cast Bohdi in the role of villain. Handsome, unrepentant, distracting villain. Bohdi had been in the role of bad guy for so long now, what did one more week matter?

Alex glanced down at her laptop, then over at her phone. At some point she was going to change that password. *Bohdi Vonn is 100% infuriating* is what it should be. Alex laughed out loud. She wasn't leaving until she did. That would serve him right.

She pulled up her email, disheartened by the number of unread messages. She had literally cleared it this morning. Alex couldn't pinpoint when she'd become so disillusioned with her work. Probably when she made the decision to contract out. She was making three times her previous salary, but it was demanding. Her time was spent reviewing the financials of mergers between companies. Owners and CEOs never liked to wait when money was on the line. But Alex was the best, and her dance card was always full. Too full.

Alex closed her computer. She needed a distraction, and one that did not include Bohdi. The sea salt caverns had been a new addition to the resort a year or two ago. The theory was it would help with high blood pressure and improve lung function. The negatively charged ions in salt were also supposed to improve one's mood. That would be useful right about now. As long as Bohdi remained on site, Alex knew she needed all the help she could get controlling her blood pressure and the quickening of her breath when he was around.

She still had plenty of time to review the numbers. Talisman wasn't an overly complicated organization. Cal and her father didn't have vast holdings to search through. The resort was all they shared. It would be a simple matter to run through things before the representatives from RG Holdings arrived. Besides, there shouldn't be any surprises. Alex really was embracing avoidance.

Alex got up to grab a snack and while she was rifling through the refrigerator, she noticed a red flashing coming from a table in the hall. The landline! It was so obvious now. She wondered if Cal had left a message. He had been both eager and concerned about the sale. She knew she needed to have a strategic meeting with him. This morning didn't quite go as she planned.

Alex's stomach clenched as she listened to the message. Arlo must have called after she left. He apologized for not asking when they had spoken but informed her that they were saving a seat for her at their table for the silent auction tonight at the T-Bar. He was sending Gus to pick her up.

Arlo was smart. If he had asked her in person, he knew she would have found a way to decline the invitation. But a message without a return number and a pre-planned escort was far more difficult to dodge. Perhaps she should be grateful he wasn't sending Bohdi.

The idea of the sea salt caverns seemed a necessity now. Alex was going to go, decompress, and face this evening with a smile. She would enjoy her time with Freda and Arlo, do her best to tolerate Bohdi, and then come home. After a good night's sleep, she would be back to business tomorrow.

***

The T-Bar was shut down for the afternoon in preparation for the evening's silent auction. Bohdi marvelled at how quickly Mick and Jaz had pulled things together. At times they could make his job incredibly easy.

The hotel kitchen was providing all the hors d'oeuvres, so once the tables, easels, and sound system were set up; they were essentially ready to go. Bohdi was carrying out the last easel when he saw Mick and Jaz sitting on the bar stools, watching him.

He placed it with the others and walked over to the siblings.

'What?' he asked.

Jaz shrugged. 'You tell us. We just spent an hour shuffling things around and not one word from you about your not-so-mysterious stranger.'

He should have known better than to think he would escape their interrogation. He had been pleasantly surprised when all conversation had been solely on the tasks at hand.

'Not much to say—'

'Not much to say?' exclaimed Jaz. 'I bloody disagree. Your intriguing lady on the road, the one you could barely wait to meet, turns out to be Jim's daughter, the woman who plans on selling this place to the highest bidder. And you stand here claiming there's not much to say.' Jaz shook her head with disgust. 'The Bohdi I know would have heaps to say.'

Bohdi watched as Jaz crossed her arms and waited for a response. What did she want him to say? That since Cal mentioned that Alex agreed to sell Talisman, he had been feeling lost? Exactly like he had felt up until the moment Jim Mason had offered him the opportunity to open the T-Bar. That he was unsure of where life was heading? And that seeing Alex again was only adding to his uncertainty? That his dead best friend's little sister had bowled him over and he didn't know how to get back up? Bohdi didn't even want to think it and he sure as hell wasn't going to say it out loud. He glanced to Mick, who seemed to take pity.

'I don't know, Bohdi. She seemed nice, pretty sweet, really.' Mick looked to his sister. 'Not what I expected, I guess.'

'Not what I expected either,' Bohdi agreed.

'So?' Jaz demanded. 'What does that mean? Because whoever she is, regardless of what you expected, she's what we've got. Do you think we have a problem here?'

'I'm not sure what to think, Jaz,' replied Bohdi.

'I'm asking if you think you can convince her to not sell.'

'I know what you're asking, Jaz. I can't give you answers I don't have.'

Jaz liked to face challenges head on. It had done her well in the past, but Arlo had been right: Alex Mason might require a little more finesse. Jim's daughter may think she was pure logic and rational, but Bohdi had a feeling that the wild child who fought like a demon when backed into a corner was hiding in there still. How long could a person deny their true self?

'Why does she want to sell, anyway? I know that Cal checked out a while ago, but why does she need to toss her stake?'

Mick asked a good question. Bohdi just wasn't sure which answer was the right one.

'She hasn't been here in a long time. I doubt she feels any connection to the mountain anymore. She also has some pretty sad memories of this place. I can't fault her for those.'

Bohdi didn't need to explain the effect Ben's death could have on his sister. They already knew what it had done to Bohdi. But maybe it was more than Ben. Her mother had been the polar opposite of her father. That must have played a role in who she was now.

'Her mother left. Didn't want to be so far from the city. It probably seemed exciting here for a while, but Elizabeth Mason was a socialite and grew tired of watching the jet set crowd leave here without her. After their divorce, she took Alex to live with her. So maybe that's all Alex knows.'

Even saying the words, his heart was heavy. He hoped he was wrong. Bohdi didn't like to think of Alex, her spirit stifled in the confines of her mother's social circles. Somewhere, even if deep inside, Alex had to remember what it was like to feel the freedom of the mountain.

'Maybe you can chat her up? Remind her of the magic that brings people from all over the world here.'

Mick didn't seem to realize it wasn't that easy.

Bohdi sighed, 'I can hardly get her to talk with me, never mind enough time alone, to make a convincing argument.'

Jaz suddenly straightened, looking from her brother to Bohdi. 'Good point, you're both on the mark.'

'What does that mean?' Bohdi asked. He didn't like it when Jaz got that look in her eyes.

She spun around off the stool and smiled, as she smacked Bohdi's arm with the palm of her hand. 'Doesn't mean anything. Mick's right. You're Mr. Charming, and you need the chance to talk to her.'

Bohdi bit his bottom lip as he sized up Jaz. He turned to Mick, who simply shrugged with his 'don't ask me' face.

Jaz moved towards the door. 'Look good here, yeah? Do I have time for a few runs?'

She was changing the subject, but Bohdi knew that it was always better to let Jaz burn off some energy. She was dangerously creative, and liable to find trouble if given a chance.

'Go. We're good.' Bohdi sent her out the door. He turned back to look at Mick.

'Should I be worried?' he asked.

'Will it help?' said Mick.

Bohdi didn't bother to respond. They both knew the answer to that question.

***

Alex sifted the warm salt between her toes. She leaned back in the half lounger that was wedged into the loose grains of salt a foot deep on the floor. The heat enveloped her, and if she didn't peek to see the dim glow of the salt lamp fireplace, she could almost pretend that she was on a beach somewhere. A place where blue eyes and blonde hair were replaced by a sexy thick accent and the dark skin and hair of a man named Armando, who was bringing her a drink from the open bar.

She growled as Armando insisted on wearing a ski pants and kept laughing as he offered her a glass of scotch that was mostly ice. Fantastic, now his eyes matched the pristine waters behind him. You suck, Armando.

Attempting to purge thoughts of Bohdi from her mind was proving more difficult than she imagined. The low lighting and soothing music were relaxing. It gave Alex some time to reflect on recent events. Alex couldn't remember a time she had completely unplugged. If she wasn't working, she was attending whichever function her mother deemed important for her. She hated all of them. She went because it was easier than fighting with her mother. When had she become so afraid of confrontation?

Earlier, when her phone had exploded with urgent notifications of trivial concerns, it was another sign that it was time for a change. Alex usually addressed each issue as it arrived, and when she saw the backlog of barely one day's disengagement, she realized how much of her days and nights were wrapped up in everyone else's problems. *I guess if you're busy solving the difficulties of others, you never have to focus on your own.*

The caverns claimed that 45 minutes of this halotherapy was the equivalent of three days on the beach. Alex contemplated staying for a few more hours. She was starting to settle in when two other women arrived.

They spoke softly, but the space was still small. She kept her eyes closed, thankful acknowledgement wasn't required. Alex almost drifted off to sleep, when she heard the name Bohdi in their chat.

Hating herself for doing so, but unable to prevent it, Alex nonchalantly began to eavesdrop on their conversation.

'No one will be able to outbid me. I'm certain to win.'

Win? What were they talking about?

'You're not the only one with deep pockets, Cassandra. He's the hottest prize they have. I wouldn't even bother attending if he wasn't on the menu.'

The two ladies softly laughed. 'Well we'll see who wins a date with Bohdi Vonn. To the victor go the spoils.'

The women giggled again, and Alex could picture them clinking champagne flutes in mutual admiration for their clever musings.

So Bohdi had placed himself on the auction block. It absolutely figured. The man's arrogance knew no bounds. From the conversation she had heard, he may be justified in thinking he could raise a few dollars. She truly had stepped into the *Bohdi Vonn Variety Show*. It was almost enough reason to back out of going. It was a silent auction, so that would at least save her from watching the female guests of Talisman screaming out their bids when Bohdi came up for grabs. Seriously, only a man would see nothing wrong with putting himself up for sale. No, she would go tonight, if only to see what sort of price tag was attached to Bohdi's celebrity.

Thinking about the auction made Alex realize that she needed time to get ready. It was at this moment that Alex had never been more thankful for the lessons that her mother had instilled in her early on. Always pack for every occasion. One knock-out dress and a pair of Manolos for any occasion. She didn't imagine the auction was a black tie, otherwise it would have been held in the hotel instead of Bohdi's pub. But his pub wasn't typical bar design either. You wouldn't find a large center stone fireplace and thick, exposed wood beams surrounded by ornate carvings in your average city bar. Alex was sure that was thanks in part to her father's vision.

Yes, she had the perfect outfit on hand. She couldn't explain the desire, but she couldn't deny it either. Alex planned on showing Bohdi that she was no longer the little girl who thought he walked on water. The years were long past where he could flash that pearly white smile, gaze at her with his piercing blue eyes, and she would agree to do his bidding. She wasn't 13 anymore. She was going to slide on that dress, and slip into those heels, and show him how much she had grown up.

***

The friendly girls working reception at the spa were tripping over themselves to help Bohdi when he and Chewie arrived to pick up the certificate for the spa package for the silent auction. Their youthful admiration was a soothing balm to his recently bruised ego, but nothing more. At 35, he was long past the giggles of girls. Sixteen years earlier, he and Ben could have happily spent the afternoon here, working their magic. Ben would never age, but time moved on for Bohdi.

They had been fussing over and feeding treats to Chewie when the heavy wooden door that led to the caverns opened. Heat with the fragrance of a salty sea breezed through. Alex followed. She didn't see him immediately and Bohdi stood still, taking in the moment before she became aware.

She had become a beautiful woman. It was easier to appreciate when she wasn't scowling in his direction. But even scowling, she had the ferocious beauty of an animal that had been caged too long. He wondered what it took for her to rein in the wild child he remembered and maintain such control. It must be exhausting.

'Bohdi!' She was surprised to see him, and a soft blush touched her cheeks. A vision of being the one to have put that flush there instead of the warm caverns briefly crossed his mind. He pictured himself inside the salt rooms with Alex, enjoying the warmth, kissing her lips, unwrapping her—

'Woof!' Chewie's greeting cut off the depraved downward spiral of his thoughts.

'Hi, Chewie. Who's a good boy?'

Bohdi watched with unexplained jealousy as she planted kisses on top of his dog's head, who in return licked the side of her neck, enjoying the salt on her skin. Lucky dog.

'Hi, Alex.'

She stood up, still rubbing the top of Chewie's head with her fingers. 'Hello again, Bodhi.'

'I'm just here to grab this,' he held up the envelope in his hand.

'Another hot prize for the auction tonight?' she asked.

Alex didn't smile when she posed the question, but Bohdi was certain he saw a glint of laughter in the golden flecks of her hazel eyes. He wasn't sure he liked the idea of her laughing at him. Had she discovered that he was one of the items in the silent auction? He had no reason to be embarrassed. This was all for a good cause. A really good cause.

'You could say that.' Bohdi was trying very hard to remember Arlo's advice. But it was proving to be a monumental task. He was close to breaking when she excused herself.

‘I should go.’ She turned to the girls. ‘Thank you so much. It was wonderful. Almost as good as a real beach.’

‘I need to go too.’ He waved the certificate. ‘Thanks, ladies.’

When he held open the door for Alex, she placed her hand on the handle at the same time. She quickly drew back as if burned and looked up to his face. She opened her mouth as though she were going to speak, then closed it abruptly, having thought better of the idea. As she walked out, Chewie started to follow. Bohdi stuck his foot out. ‘Don’t even think about it.’

Chewie looked up at him, with what could only be doggie devastation. Bohdi shook his head in disgust. ‘Couple pieces of cheese and a few kisses, and you’re ready to leave your old life behind?’ Chewie whined and looked to where Alex was headed.

‘Yeah, yeah, buddy. You and me both.’

CHAPTER SEVEN

The steamy breath of the Percheron pulling the pretty Albany cutter rose in a cloud into cool night air. There was a brief moment when the sleigh arrived that Alex debated getting in. It all seemed a little silly. Her father had added the sleigh rides a few years back, hoping it would provide a magical feel to Talisman's winter wonderland. They had a full stable and a number of small and large sleighs, depending on whether you were looking for a rollicking ride for the family or a more romantic excursion for two.

Tucked in under the warm, exquisitely woven blankets next to Gus, her driver, Alex supposed she should be grateful that Arlo hadn't sent Bohdi on a single horse instead. This was perfectly cozy. She was pleased that her father had stopped using fur long ago and that the replacements felt just as decadent and luxurious. When Gus brought out the jingle bells and attached them to the side of the sleigh, Alex stopped him with a laugh.

'I don't need the announcement, Gus.'

'It's not for you, Miss Mason, it's for Sophie.' He nodded to his horse. 'She enjoys the attention.'

Alex couldn't argue. She didn't have a vast knowledge of horses, but there was no doubting that Sophie was a beauty and the horse knew it. Her coat was shining in the moonlight and she held her head high as they made the short ride.

'She certainly deserves it. She's lovely,' conceded Alex. Bells it was.

She had to admit there was something wonderful about cutting through the snow in a lantern-lit sleigh, staring at the snow-capped mountains with a background of starry skies. Her father truly had designed a dream. She could only imagine how thrilled the guests were to dash through meadows of crystal snow and thick evergreens, then cross the frozen lake to the east of the property. Each trip would finish with an elaborate fondue to the delight of the guests. It was the perfect way to complete a day of fantasy. Her father thought of everything. It was also why he never wanted to expand the village. He was creating an experience, not simply a place to ski. Alex wished the ride would last a little longer. But she could only put off her evening for so long and unless she was willing to confess her cowardice to Gus, it was time for her to get out.

As Gus pulled up to the T-Bar, Alex realized that she still needed to get across the snow to reach the stone pathways that led to the pub's entrance. Her Manolos would never make it. She looked to Gus with momentary panic.

'I don't think I thought this through, Gus.' Alex pulled up the blankets to reveal her fabulous, but impractical, heels.

Gus jumped down from the cutter, laughing as he came to her side. For one horrified moment Alex pictured Gus carrying her into the pub, ensuring her evening began with complete humiliation. Instead, he reached under the seat behind her.

'Don't worry, Miss Mason, your father never forgot the details.' He pulled out a rolled-up mat and he flung it out in front of the cutter, where it granted safe passage to the pathway.

'Of course he didn't,' she chuckled, placing her fingers in Gus's extended palm.

'Every lady deserves to walk the red carpet, at least once.'

'Thank you so much, Gus, this has been lovely.' Alex almost felt the need to curtsy to Gus's gallant bow. 'I guess I will see you later tonight?'

'Yes, Miss. Have a nice time.'

Alex's bravado disappeared along with Gus. It was chilly outside, but not quite enough to propel her in. It was only the laughter of a well-dressed group of people coming up the walkway that prompted Alex to move. She was feeling quite clever in her plan to conceal her arrival by casually entering with the crowd.

An enthusiastic young man borrowed from the hotel staff gave her an appreciative smile as he took her coat at the door. Alex thanked him as she straightened her shoulders and walked in, searching for the familiar faces of Freda and Arlo. If she was here at their behest, she hoped that they had already arrived. The place was packed with people dressed to impress. Once again, Alex silently thanked her mother. Elizabeth Mason was many things, but unprepared was never one of them.

Arlo's waving hand caught her eye and Alex made her way to their table. Alex did not recognize the two other instructors that joined them. But then again, why would she? She wasn't a part of this place anymore. Introductions were made and, with a quick glance about the pub, she sat down.

'You look beautiful, Ally,' said Freda.

'Thank you, Freda. Everyone here seems to have cleaned up rather nicely as well.'

'It's Alex now; she not a little girl anymore,' reminded Arlo.

'I can see that, Arlo, my eyesight hasn't left me yet—'

‘It’s alright,’ Alex smiled at the confusion her name was causing. ‘Ally is fine. I promise I will still answer to it.’ Alex quickly changed the subject. ‘Looks like there is a great turnout. What is the benefit for?’

Freda jumped in, eager to speak. ‘About four years ago, we started a Para-Alpine Club. Back in Austria, it was introduced after the Second World War. There was a lack of options for differently abled people in our sport. There still is, but not here! Oh, it has been a wonderful success. We’ve even expanded to include a rogue snowboarder or two.’ She looked to Arlo with a wink. He rolled his eyes in return. ‘It’s been fantastic. With the regular ski program essentially running itself, we wanted to create something special. Do more for our sport.’

Freda’s eyes lit up as she talked about the program. It was obvious to the whole table that she had found her passion. It warmed her to see Freda so excited. Alex wished that passion would spill over into her own line of work.

‘That’s wonderful, Freda. What a great idea. Besides,’ Alex gave Arlo a nudge with her shoulder, ‘It gives this guy an extra set of students to intimidate.’

Arlo grumped under his breath, but Alex could tell he was still pleased she could remember.

She delighted in listening to the stories from all parties at her table. Tales of the day’s events and behind-the-scenes gossip found Alex laughing freely for the first time in longer than she cared to remember. Freda and Arlo recounted her personal tales of mischief and, despite momentary embarrassment, Alex discovered she was truly enjoying the evening. It was almost disconcerting to feel so relaxed. She hadn’t expected it.

Even with the pleasant company, Alex kept scanning the room. The harder she tried to not look for Bohdi, the more she did. It’s like being told to not think about a delicious cake; no matter what, it only guarantees that you do. Of course, Bohdi was neither delicious or edible, but he was stuck in her mind. Yes, she definitely needed to keep one eye out for Bohdi. If only so that she was prepared when he did appear. Forewarned is forearmed. Not that she was going to battle. She was only planning in case of a skirmish.

'He's over there.' Freda pointed to the back corner of the pub. 'You'll have to turn around.'

Alex did her best to feign surprise. 'Who?'

Freda smiled, exchanging a look with Arlo, and said, 'Bohdi.'

'Oh no,' Alex brushed away Freda's silly observation. 'I'm certainly not looking for Bohdi. I was just admiring the interior here. The work is spectacular.'

Seriously, that was what she came up with? Spectacular architecture. No wonder Freda was looking at her like that.

'Yes, a real piece of work.' Freda's knowing smile floated across the table. 'It was quite a collaboration between Jim and Bohdi. I know they enjoyed working together immensely.'

'Oh, good,' replied Alex. What was she supposed to say?

Well, she wasn't going to turn around, that was for sure. Especially when Freda was looking at her, expecting her to do exactly that. Nope, she was not turning around to look at Bohdi Vonn. Freda looked disappointed, but not deterred.

'There is some lovely woodwork, over your shoulder there. Have you ever seen anything quite so handsome?'

Freda knew exactly what she was doing, and Alex was losing her fight with restraint. If only to appease the woman, Alex quickly glanced over her shoulder. Then peeked again.

Ughh. No, she hadn't seen anything so handsome. But then that was the point, wasn't it? The formal tuxedo was a bit over the top for the evening. This wasn't a black-tie affair. Bohdi should look out of place, but he didn't. Why didn't that surprise her? He had also placed himself up for sale this evening and wanted to get top dollar. The man certainly knew how to market himself.

Well, she looked good too. No, she looked fantastic. It wasn't a competition, but if it were, she was definitely in the running. Alex had taken every care when she got ready earlier this evening. She even had the ladies at the hotel salon style her hair and apply her make-up. Their assistance had been invaluable, as Alex's nerves were making it difficult to hold even a tube of lipstick. She should not have been in such a tizzy, but it seemed her logical side was slipping by the hour. There had been several moments of self-doubt, but when she finally slid into the snug bottle-green dress and looked in the mirror, she had been pleased. It's said that the color green is one of temptation. It had not been her intent when she had packed the outfit, but if highlighting her every curve could assist her in gaining the upper hand with Bohdi, who was she to argue? *Use the weapons in your arsenal*, another bit of Elizabeth Mason advice. Usually Alex managed relying solely on her quick wit and reasoning, but maybe when Bohdi saw her as a woman in her own right, he would forget about the little girl who at one time would have granted his every wish.

Now that she had seen Bohdi, she wasn't so sure that would be enough. He had an air of confidence that only came from a life where each desire was easily filled. Alex was sure he was used to getting what he wanted. And wearing the tuxedo instead of a simple suit, please, he was practically shouting to the world, 'Look at me! Celebrity Bohdi Vonn.'

Well, it wasn't going to work on her. Yes, he was an attractive man, but Alex barely noticed the perfect cut of his jacket, and the way his pants hugged him in all the right places. He may look good, but he was no James Bond. More like an evil villain, comfortable in his lair and she was trapped inside. She needed to get a grip.

Alex looked purposefully away from Bohdi and checked out the rest of the evening's patrons. There was no doubt that there was a lot of money in this crowd. Talisman was obviously still bringing in upscale clientele. That was a good thing, as Freda's program was deserving of support. It was interesting that, despite the flush crowd ready to part with their money for a good cause, it felt nothing like the charitable functions she attended with her mother in the city. It didn't feel like the cold collection of coin from one's peers. It felt like a community. It felt good. From the corner of her eye, Alex saw a familiar face headed her way.

'Mick! It's nice to see you again. You're going to be busy tonight!'

The charming bartender grinned. 'Yeah, but heaps of tips tonight.' He gave her an approving look. 'You're looking sharp!'

'You too,' she laughed as Mick held out his tie and spun around, showing off his striped charcoal suit.

The young man then leaned towards her, his hand on the back of her chair. 'I see they've tailored a prize just for you.'

Alex's eyes widened. If Mick dared to say Bohdi's name, she might strangle him with his flashy tie. There was nothing anyone could do to convince her to bid on him. She tried to affect an even tone and did not look up as she spoke. 'Which prize is that exactly?'

'Lovely bottle of 50-year-old Dalmore Scotch'

Arlo gave a low whistle. Alex unclenched the edge of her seat and met Mick's innocent gaze.

'I fear that might be wasted on me.'

'Bottle that pricey, I think the point's not to drink it. So perfect, yeah?' he said giving her a conspiratorial wink. 'Gotta run!'

'You've already met Mick, I see.' Freda smiled at the back of the retreating bartender. 'Have you met his twin sister Jaz as well?'

Still laughing at the cheeky young man, she replied, 'No, not yet.'

'She's Bohdi's right hand. Ahh!' Freda pointed. 'Over there.'

Alex looked to where Freda was indicating to find a whirlwind of activity in the form of young woman. She was tiny, but like Freda, looked like she could hold her own. She was animatedly conversing with several guests and had their complete attention. Jaz had one of those smiles, like a girl who knows a secret. It figured that Bohdi would surround himself with beautiful women. He probably needed them to feed his fragile ego, constantly.

Bohdi was working his way around the room and Alex found her eyes following him despite her best efforts. Bohdi was in his element, of that there was no doubt. She watched him interacting with the crowd. He knew how to connect with people. He always had. It was that charismatic pull that had likely won him all those endorsements when he had never won a gold medal. She knew all about it; she had once fallen for it too. He obviously loved what he was doing and was relishing his role as famous barkeep. Another example of how he always landed on his feet. Alex wondered if a career change of her own would be as fulfilling.

She loved the precise manner of her work. Things were black and white, columns and order. There were times when illegal lines were crossed, and people believed they were in a grey area. But that was actually black and white too. Right or wrong. In recent years a lot of her contracts had taken more of a forensic bent. There was no shortage of unscrupulous businessmen, and when companies merged these practices often came to light. Nothing remained hidden under Alex's investigative eyes. Her reputation grew and she became one of the foremost authorities in her field. It helped that she had essentially shunned a personal life for the past several years.

At first Alex enjoyed the hunt. She loved to find the secrets that CEOs and owners thought they could hide. But it was beginning to take a toll. Her findings often influenced the direction of billions of dollars when mergers fell apart. Not everyone was pleased with how thorough she was. Many were hostile and vocal in their displeasure. Alex was tired. Tired of underhanded play and companies fighting for more, when they already had more than enough. Her work ceased to be rewarding. The numbers that once brought her comfortable predictability, no longer brought her joy.

Alex didn't want a change. She needed a change. Maybe a nice island somewhere. She could handle the books for the local surf and fishing shops. Her greatest concern would be making sure the taxes were filed on time.

She needed to be drowning in eyes the color of molasses and short swimming trunks, not staring at pools of blue and a perfectly fitted tux.

***

Bohdi could feel her eyes on him.

He noticed her the moment she tried to slip inconspicuously through the door. She might have eluded detection if he hadn't been watching for her all night.

When she stepped out from the group, he felt his mouth go dry. She was stunning. If he had wondered what her legs were like, he certainly wondered no more. Her dress hit barely above the knee, but clung to her every curve, like a roadmap to satisfaction. She had the body of an athlete and the face of an angel. Her blonde tresses were loose around her shoulders, instead of the thick braid that she had worn earlier today. She didn't show much décolleté; she didn't need too. She was all class and sensuality. Her dress, like the woman who wore it, only hinted at what was beneath, but gave nothing away. It reflected her perfectly. But Bohdi's imagination was more than sufficient and his trousers were becoming tighter. Alexandra Mason had turned from a gangly girl into a dangerously appealing adversary. And that was exactly what she was. He needed to look away. His mind was going down the wrong track. There was no light at the end of that tunnel.

Multiple times he had to stop himself from approaching her. Bohdi knew Arlo would be less than impressed if he were to run over to Alex and act on the wicked visions playing out in his head.

No, first he must gather his thoughts. He needed to refrain from wishful thinking and cool the fire that was building inside him. Bohdi had barely heard a word of what anyone said to him since Alex had waltzed in. Once he got the rapid beating of his heart under control, he would approach her. And he would behave. At least he would try.

But Bohdi could feel her eyes on him, so he willed himself not to turn around. Focus on whatever this guest and his lovely wife were discussing and not on what it would feel like to run his hands along the side of Alex's neck and through her hair. He willed his body not to respond to his wicked thoughts. It wasn't working. He needed to face this problem head on, before he embarrassed himself in front of the sweet couple he had been chatting with.

He excused himself and moved through the crowd towards Alex, the collar of his tuxedo starting to tighten with every step and the temperature of the room seemed to be rising as well. He was being ridiculous. Alex was no different than any of the beautiful women in this room. Except that was a lie, and he knew it the moment he had met her on the road. She was different. She was familiar and unknown territory all wrapped into one confusing, gorgeous package. For the first time in his life Bohdi was at a loss how to proceed. Women had never been difficult for him. Maybe that was because he was never invested. But this time, this woman, she was the key to his happiness, his mountain. And she was far from happy with him. He wanted her to remember he was not the enemy, and that there was much that they shared. Good memories along with the bad. He really needed to keep his tongue in check.

'Evening, nice to see everyone in their finery.'

Bohdi took great pains to look at everyone at the table as he spoke. His eyes may have rested a moment too long on Alex, as her cheeks quickly developed a rosy hue. He was certain his lusty thoughts had been pushed to the deepest recesses of his mind, but Alex was reacting like she could read them. What if she could? What would she think? What would she do?

When she met his gaze through her long lashes, Bohdi could have sworn her eyes were now green, a reflection of her dress. But when her earrings caught the light, they seemed to match the specks of gold staring at him. If the woman's eye color could change on a whim, should he be surprised about her moods?

Arlo cleared his throat, and Bohdi blinked. 'Right. You look rather fetching in your dress, Alex.'

See, he could be chivalrous. There was no way Arlo could find fault in that. No one could find insult or innuendo in as innocuous a word as fetching. Score one point for Bohdi.

The corner of Alex's mouth quivered slightly. Was she going to smile?

'Thank you, Bohdi. You look rather dapper yourself.'

Ahh, they were both going to play nice. A point on the board for Alex. Freda looked pleased at their interaction.

'I'm actually surprised you had something to wear. Such a short trip and all. All business, no pleasure.' Bohdi couldn't stop himself from talking. Why was he still talking? 'Guess you can't take the city out—'

Bohdi clamped his lips together to hold back his scream as Arlo ground the heel of his size 15 shoe into the top of Bohdi's right toe, under the table.

Through clenched teeth he amended his comment. 'Sorry, that may have come out wrong. What I meant was I am pleasantly surprised to see you had something so perfectly appropriate to wear.' Bohdi gave a sigh of relief when Arlo released his foot.

'And I'm surprised you feel the need to catalogue my wardrobe, or maybe I shouldn't be surprised,' a forced smile on her face, Alex continued. 'You seem to be very good at involving yourself in things that aren't your concern.' Her eyes bored into him, challenging him to respond.

'I think I have plenty to be concerned about, so I guess it's up for debate.'

Alex scoffed, 'There's no debate.'

Bohdi watched the narrowing of Alex's eyes and the lift of her chin. Although he longed to respond, he also valued his ability to walk for the rest of the evening and decided to change tack.

'So, we have a great turnout. You see anything you like?'

'Not yet.' Alex didn't even crack a smile, but the small flicker across her face gave her away. Oh, now she thought she was clever.

'Ouch! I feel that was directed at me. Although that wouldn't make sense, as I know I look good tonight. Even Chewie respected my *dapper* look. See? Not a single hair on me!' He slowly spun around to make his point. 'So, I'll assume you haven't taken the time to look around.'

'I hope this isn't an indication of the quality of the items?' Alex waved a bored hand in his direction.

Bohdi leaned forward, placing his hands on the table. ‘Perhaps you’d like to test that quality yourself, before you make any big decisions.’

‘You think—’

Arlo interrupted with a cough and Bohdi moved his foot out of reach. Bohdi hadn’t even noticed that the rest of their company had disappeared. The big Austrian then stood, glaring at both of them. ‘Pfft. Good luck. I’m going to look for less aggravating company and a prize in my price range. One of those shouldn’t be too hard to find.’

Bohdi slid into Arlo’s empty seat, moving it closer to Alex. She folded her arms, refusing to look at him. He glanced briefly at the rise of her breasts, pushed up by angry forearms. He didn’t want to argue with Alex, but he couldn’t deny this one benefit.

‘Well, we can certainly clear a table.’ He gave her delicate ear his best apologetic smile.

Alex was biting her bottom lip, perhaps as a reminder to bite her tongue. Then she exhaled and eased back in her chair.

‘I guess we can.’ Her hazel eyes finally turned to him. ‘Look, Bohdi, I don’t want to be at odds with you the entire time I’m here. It’s only a week, and then I’m gone. Once the deal is complete, I will be out of your life, forever.’

Bohdi wasn’t sure he could determine which part of that last statement he disliked the most. ‘The sale is a definite go?’

‘Why wouldn’t it be?’

‘I don’t know, Alex. I thought maybe if you spent some time here you would remember how wonderful it is.’

‘I don’t want to remember, Bohdi. This part of my life is over. I need it to be over. Why would you want to prevent me from moving on? Even with the sale you will still have your pub, your life here. Nothing will change.’

'Nothing will change? Is that what you believe? You think a company like RG Holdings, and yes, I know exactly who they are, wants a boutique resort in the mountains? No way, Alex. They don't care about the experience, or the magic of Talisman. They care about a bottom line, and that means levelling the forest that surrounds us to build endless rows of condos and lodges. Nothing will change? Everything will change.'

Alex shook her head. 'That's not true. Cal promised me they had no interest in overdevelopment. Talisman is profitable the way it is. There is no need to expand the way you are talking. The mountain would lose all its cachet. Why would they?'

'Because companies don't care about cachet. They care about cash. You're smart, Alex, you know it's true.'

'You're not basing this on fact; you're making assumptions. I don't work that way. I'm sorry, Bohdi. It's time for me to move on. You certainly have,' said Alex.

'What is that supposed to mean?'

'Nothing. It doesn't mean anything. I'm only saying that you're going to be fine. You always are.'

There was something she wasn't telling him. It was in her eyes, but not in her words. He didn't know what it was, but whatever it was, it was affecting her decision process. Then again, maybe there was no process. Maybe she made up her mind long before she came back to Talisman. Maybe he was a fool to think he even had a chance.

'You know what, Alex? You should go take a look at the prizes. Somewhere over there are two tickets to anywhere in the world. Sounds like just the thing for someone like you.'

When he saw the hurt in her eyes at his words, he wished he could take them back. But it was too late; she blinked and all expression was gone. It was a master class in self-control. She pushed herself up from the table.

'Sounds perfect. I guess I'll go do that.'

Bohdi watched as Alex walked away from him. It was a vision he'd better get used to.

CHAPTER EIGHT

Alex slowly strolled along the wall of auction items, perusing each certificate on the easels provided. She didn't know why it irritated her so much that Bohdi said the tickets would suit her. They would. Wasn't that exactly what she wanted? Why was she bothered when Bohdi said she should keep her share of Talisman and then insulted when he told her to do exactly what she wanted to? This whole place had her turned upside down.

When she reached the bidding sheet for the plane tickets, she looked over her shoulder. Bohdi's eyes were still on her. She lifted the pen and, on impulse, wiggled it in his direction. He acknowledged her with a nod, but he didn't smile. She wrote down her name. He was irritating, but he was right. She needed to stay focused on the task at hand, not on the uncomfortable feelings that Bohdi was creating, in both her body and her mind.

There was an open stool near the back bar, so Alex walked over to take it. She needed a breather from the crowd, and she needed a drink.

'Alex!' Mick looked over, ready to take her order. 'What'll you have?'

'Glass of wine would be lovely, Mick.'

'Of?'

'Surprise me,' she answered.

The lines in his forehead creased as Mick's eyes darted out to the room before them. 'Glad you like surprises.'

It was an odd statement. But Mick was busy, so she didn't have time to question him before Freda began to address the crowd. Podium below and microphone in hand, the short woman was still barely level to the gathering before her.

Freda welcomed everyone and thanked them for their time and their money, as she explained the importance of the Para Alpine Program. Her passion was evident, and her energy invigorated the crowd. Alex was enjoying her wine and observing the well-heeled group, when Freda's words caught her attention.

'Like our own Jaz. Wave, Jaz!' Freda smiled at the girl, as Jaz gave a friendly wave to everyone. 'Our funds, funds raised by wonderful people such as yourselves, paid for Jaz to train through the International Paralympic Committee. Jaz plans on representing us in six years on the National Para Snowboarding Team. You can all thank yourselves… and Jaz,' she winked, 'when she brings home gold.'

There was a hearty round of applause from everyone. Freda knew exactly how to work this crowd. They liked to help, but they loved gratitude and validation. Both were easy to give and worth every penny.

Alex was impressed. It took dedication to achieve in any sport and Jaz was clearly a testament to hard work mixed with talent. It was also a reminder to Alex of how blind she could be at times. She had been watching Jaz. It was only to learn a little about the attractive young woman who was Bohdi's right hand, of course. She assumed that Jaz was one of those lucky girls who had a natural sexy sway to her walk. The throng of people had been too thick for her to see that Jaz had a prosthetic from the knee down on her left leg. There must be some truth to the saying that you only see what you want to see. Never missed a number that was out of place, but when it came to people? Oblivious.

She looked over to Mick and raised a brow. He slid a drink to the man in front of him and then came over.

'Impressive,' she said.

Mick shrugged. 'She can be a pain, straight up. But there's no one tougher. Once she gets something in her head, it's stuck. She only knows flat out.'

'Lot to be said for perseverance, not everyone has it. You must be proud of her.'

'I am, usually,' he replied. 'She does have some crazy moments though.'

He was searching the room again and Alex noticed when Mick caught his sister's eye. They exchanged glances. When Mick rubbed the back of his neck at Jaz's sly smile, Alex was certain she was missing something. Why wasn't expression quantifiable?

'She must be a big help to Bohdi, then?' she asked.

'We'll see.'

Mick quickly moved off to the other end of the bar, busying himself with anything that didn't include making eye contact with her. Alex didn't bother pursuing it. She had plenty to worry about that didn't include divining secrets between brother and sister.

When Cal arrived, Alex went over to greet him. He asked if she had reviewed the financial statements for Talisman yet, and when she told she hadn't, he sighed audibly and finished his drink in one swallow. Alex attributed his behaviour to nerves. Cal had been holding the fort for a while, and Alex didn't blame him for being anxious. She had often seen that reaction from the accountants in companies that hired her. It was like seeing the police in your review mirror. You know you haven't committed a crime, but your heart beats a little faster anyway. He was happy with her reassurances about the potential deal, but soon made his excuses and left. Alex noticed he had bid on the expensive scotch before heading out the door. Cal really wasn't looking well.

Alex searched for Freda and Arlo. She wanted to continue her conversation with them. It was so nice to talk with them. She was worried they would be upset with her silence over the years, but all three of them had picked up right where they left off. If only for this reconnection, Alex was glad she came back.

Watching Bohdi work the room, no doubt to bring up his price, she noticed Jaz was over at one of the easels with two of their guests. The ladies seemed quite upset, and Jaz appeared to be the cause. It looked to turn physical, when Alex watched Jaz plaster a smile to her face, and don sad eyes. Whatever she was saying affected the two women immediately. They clutched their hands to their hearts, and sighed, hanging on to Jaz's every word. The ladies turned and left the conversation, smiles between them, while Jaz rolled her eyes heavenward.

Curiosity was getting the better of her, and Alex was about to introduce herself to Jaz, when Arlo touched her elbow.

'Come join me.'

She followed Arlo to their table, wondering if she would ever get the chance to meet the infamous Jaz. She started to speculate if there was more to Bohdi and Jaz. Alex wouldn't be surprised if there were.

'Are Bohdi and Jaz… together?'

Alex wished she could take back the words as soon as she spoke them. The corner of his mouth lifted and Arlo's brows drew together. It felt like he was looking right through her. But why? It was a simple question. Alex was sure other people had wondered the same thing.

'No, they aren't. Never have, never will.'

Arlo was looking at her as if she should explain why she wanted to know. Well, she didn't need to explain that, nor did she need to explain the sudden relief that she felt. She hated to think she was involved in anything deceitful when she planned to meet Bohdi before she knew who he really was. That was the only reason for her relief.

Alex changed the topic, hoping to avoid any further chance of embarrassment. Arlo was happy to go along. They were discussing the excitement of his impending grandchild, when an excited Freda stepped back on the podium.

She watched Arlo's face as he watched Freda speaking to the crowd. Still so in love after all these years. It was rare to see such emotional longevity, more so in the circles her mother demanded she partake in. Long marriages were often based more on politics, business, and preservation of money than love. It was touching to see a lasting love. Alex felt a twinge of sadness thinking of her future. She felt no desire to be a pawn or showpiece. It was rare if she ventured out on a second date, never mind opening her heart to an everlasting love. The odds were low that anyone would find such love, so she never took the risk. It simply wasn't worth it.

Freda announced the winners of the auctions and Alex was pleased to hear she had won the plane tickets. When her name was announced, she couldn't keep from glancing at Bohdi, who gave her a tight-lipped nod in congratulations. Alex didn't know why his reaction bothered her so much or why she even bothered to check. It shouldn't matter what Bohdi thought.

As they went through the list of winners, Alex could see Arlo was enjoying his wife's delight with the amount of money that had been raised. Freda was bouncing on her toes, excited to announce the final item. Alex couldn't deny that she was curious.

'And now for our final prize. An incredible day of deep powder heli-skiing with Mr. Bohdi Vonn. Courtesy of Peak

Tours and… Mr. Bohdi Vonn.' Freda waited as the clapping and a few whistles of appreciation died down.

Freda read the card. 'Oh! A second win! Alexandra Mason! You're the victor. What a wonderful donation! Ally! Where are you, dear?'

Cheers rang throughout the crowd, as Alex sat frozen to her chair. She whispered out of the corner of her mouth to Arlo. 'But I didn't.'

'Just raise your hand,' he whispered back.

'I don't think you understand—'

'Smile and wave, Alex. You don't want to look cheap with this crowd and we can sort it out later.'

Alex lifted her hand, a smile transfixed to her face, as she looked out at the crowd. There were several disappointed glares, but the two ladies she noticed arguing with Jaz earlier were now squeezing each other's hands and smiling at her. What was going on?

She finally saw Bohdi, his face a mask of confusion. He looked shocked, but maybe his stint in acting had served him well. He shook his head at her, as though this was somehow unexpected. Oh, he was good.

Alex sat, foot tapping like a drum keeping time under the table. Arlo didn't say a word as they sat in silence waiting for Freda to finish. Announcements complete, a very animated Freda hurried to their table, her face lit with pleasure.

'How wonderful, Alex, and such a surprise!'

'Sure is.'

Freda agreed. 'I know! There were so many that were vying for Bohdi tonight. And to think that it was you that won! How fortunate!'

'A veritable miracle, Freda.' Alex rose from the table. 'If you will excuse me for a moment, I believe I need to work out some details.'

'Of course, I can come with you, if you like?'

Alex saw Arlo place his large hand over his wife's. 'How about you stay right here with me, love.' As Freda was looking at Arlo in question, Alex mouthed a thank you to him, and quickly left the table.

Alex tried to slow her breath, but her legs were marching over to Bohdi faster than she liked.

'You!' she hissed through clenched teeth. Alex didn't want to make a scene, not here, but she was a hair's breadth away from knocking out his perfect teeth, one perfect tooth at a time, starting with that stupid incisor.

'You… you… ughhh!'

***

She was like a demon possessed. He thought she might strike him down on the spot. He could see her clenching and unclenching her fists at her side, chest heaving in a ripple of green. Angry, but glorious, he fought the urge to kiss her. He was wise enough to realize Alex would not appreciate his affections at this point. He had been upset by their conversation earlier, but when they announced her name for the heli-skiing date, he felt a slight glimmer of hope.

He leaned forward, but not too close, in case she bit him.

'Why are you so angry right now? You are the one who bought me.' He breathed in her scent before he moved away. She smelled like honey and sunshine, a day at the beach, which contrasted with the dark thunderous face that was glaring at him.

'I did not.'

Bohdi thought she might stomp a foot. Her outrage was palatable.

'Well, unless there is another Alexandra Mason who thinks 30 grand is a small price to pay for all of this?'

The daggers shooting from Alex's eyes nearly caused him to step back.

'You are really unbelievable. If you think I would ever–
–'

Bohdi help up his hand. 'Whoa now. Seriously? You didn't…' His words trailed off as he looked to the back of the bar. Mick, who had been watching, quickly averted his gaze, refusing to make eye contact. He couldn't see Jaz.

When he looked back down to Alex, the muscles in her face were no longer twitching, but she still did not look pleased.

'I'm not sure what—'

'Then you may want to check with your minions,' interrupted Alex.

'Minions? That's a little strong—'

Alex cut him off again, this time grabbing his hand and turning him around. A jolt passed between them. Alex gasped and let go.

'I… I must have shocked you,' she excused.

'Alex, there's no carpet.'

'Whatever, just look.'

Did he really think that Alex was going to address what had passed between them? Of course not. Bohdi looked across to see Jaz wiggling her fingers, a great big self-satisfied smile on her face. Bohdi glared at her and Jaz winked in return.

'I'm pretty sure that she works for you, therefore…'

Bohdi couldn't argue with her logic. And he had been the one complaining to Jaz that he needed to get Alex alone. That he wanted an opportunity to remind her of Talisman's beauty and magic. He had practically spoon fed the idea to Jaz. Did he really think she wouldn't have acted? He should have known better by now. But maybe Jaz hadn't been so far off the mark. There was a chance he could turn this around.

'Listen, Alex, I didn't know about this, but maybe it's not all bad.'

Alex's jaw nearly hit the floor. 'You think I would consider going with you? Especially after this underhanded display?'

No, no he didn't, but it was still worth a shot. He needed to convince her.

'It's for a great cause, and you've already won.'

She was looking at him like he had grown a second head. 'Bohdi, I didn't even bid. Not on you, anyway. I know it's a good cause. I'll donate the money, but I am not going in that helicopter and I am not going skiing with you. Why on earth would I? Seriously, can you give me one, one GOOD reason why I should?'

She was asking for a reason, which meant there was a chance, at least he thought that was what it meant. Alex was a very confusing woman. She waited, and then turned to walk away.

'Wait!' Bohdi had one shot. 'If you want to sell Talisman so badly then shouldn't you take a good look at what you're selling? You haven't been here in a long time, Alex. A lot has changed on this mountain. You're a businesswoman. If you want to get top dollar for this place, then you better understand the goods you're hawking. It's not like Cal can take you. Come with me; there will be no better way to see and experience what you plan to sell.'

He watched as she turned his words over in her mind. He hoped she couldn't see his fingers crossed behind his back. She scrunched up her face as if she had tasted something bad.

'Ugh… fine, I'll go. But it has to be tomorrow. RG Holdings arrives the next day.'

Bohdi exhaled. 'No problem. I'll have everything ready. I'll have everything ready.'

He placed his hand on her shoulder, his fingers touching fabric and soft warm skin. 'This is good, Alex. I promise you won't regret it.'

Alex stepped back, forcing Bohdi's hand to fall away, and lifted her chin to meet his gaze.

'Bohdi, do me a favor. Don't make promises you can't keep.'

CHAPTER NINE

Why had she agreed to do this?

She had barely slept a wink and, seeing Bohdi outside on the Ski-Doo, she wasn't any further reassured that she was making the right decision. Every moment she spent with him was making her more confused. She had Bohdi Vonn in a very specific box in her mind and she didn't like his attempts to climb out.

He simply honked the horn when he arrived and waited. She thought he would come in. This morning he seemed to be taking a less aggressive approach and Alex didn't know whether to be worried or relieved. The developers were arriving tomorrow, and Alex knew she should review the financials like she had told Cal she would. She was starting to feel irresponsible that she hadn't. In her professional life, this kind of procrastination would be unacceptable, but she doubted there would be more to learn in those files than on the mountain. Bohdi was right, she needed to see how Talisman had grown, what it looked like now, and not rely on a memory that was proving to be less than accurate. At least that was the reason she was telling herself. It definitely didn't have to do with a desire to spend any time with Bohdi. She had gotten him out of her system a long time ago.

Her fluorescent jacket zipped up, Alex took one final look in the mirror. Bright lime pants and her pink jacket reflected back. Alex nodded. If they ran into problems, she would be easy to spot. Although, why she had bothered to put on make-up for a day of skiing was beyond her. Alex kissed the back of her hand to remove some of her lipstick. The last thing she needed was to draw Bohdi's attention to her lips. She definitely wouldn't be looking at his. Grabbing her helmet, she headed out the door.

Bohdi's dazzling smile almost outdid the sun peeking over the mountain ridge.

'Ready?' he asked.

'Yes, but I'll need skis and boots.'

'I've already let the shop know we're coming. Hop on.'

Bohdi gestured behind him on the sled. Alex hesitated. She was going to have to put her arms around him if she hoped to stay seated for the ride. He grinned, as if reading her mind. 'I promise I won't bite,' he said and patted the seat. 'Let's go.'

He was right, of course. There was no reason for her to pause. Wrapping her arms around the taut, tapered waist of Bohdi was absolutely no big deal. She had grown up and moved on. Yes, he was handsome, but so were lots of men and this one, well, this one would never be the one. Besides, she didn't want him to think he still had any kind of hold over her.

Throwing her leg over the seat, she tucked in behind Bohdi, running her arms under his. He gave her clasped hands a little squeeze and started up the snowmobile.

Alex stiffened. She wanted to pretend that his simple touch didn't make her catch her breath. That the slow warmth and tingle spreading through her was her excitement for the day ahead and nothing to do with the man her whole body was pressed against. She wanted to and then she didn't.

For one weak moment, Alex rested her head against Bohdi's back, as they whipped across thc snow. One moment before she once again heard the echo of her mother's warnings, when Bohdi took his left hand and held it against hers. It was a moment that lasted a little longer than it should have.

When she straightened, Alex was thankful for the roar of the engine and that, for once, Bohdi kept his mouth shut.

Once boots and powder skis were sorted out, they made their way to the helipad. Their pilot, Paul Klaas, introduced himself and outlined the plan for the day. Everything was loaded and they were soon on their way. Alex hadn't missed the new avalanche airbags he packed. Neither spoke as he attached her transceiver. He was thorough in checking all the gear. Normally the trip would have been straight up the mountain, but Alex informed Bohdi that she wanted to see the changes to Talisman, so they started with a flyover of the area instead.

Alex had seen aerial photos of Talisman before, but pictures never truly do nature justice. It was an absolutely spectacular view.

'I'm not going to lie. This is pretty incredible.'

'I'm glad you're not starting the day by lying to me,' he said and shot her a half smile. 'But yeah, there is nothing like this. Over there, see?'

Alex followed Bohdi's finger. There was a herd of elk moving through a snow-covered meadow below them. 'Wonderful! I can't remember the last time I've seen elk.' Alex looked closer. 'Is that where the sleigh rides run through? I can see a narrow cut through the trees.' She craned her neck to peer out the window. 'It looks like it runs to the resort.'

'Yup. Jim didn't want to have an overly wide path. Felt the proximity of the trees gave people a better connection to nature. Like you were back a hundred years, but still able to take a winter wonderland selfie.'

Alex didn't have to look to know that Bohdi would be smiling. She could feel the corners of her own mouth twitching too. He had always been funny; that was part of why she liked him. No, liked him then, before, not now. Why did she feel the need to remind herself of that? She needed to focus on the tour.

'Look!' she exclaimed. It was hard to keep the excitement from her voice. There was something about being able to take in all that her father had envisioned from such great heights. It was beautiful from below, but this view was extraordinary. The resort area looked like a pretty little Christmas village that people placed out on the mantle for the holidays, complete with a charming ice-skating rink around a bandstand. Alex could imagine the magic when it was lit with thousands of lights. The layout was perfect.

'It's so beautiful!' Alex smiled at Bohdi.

'It really is,' said Bohdi. But he wasn't looking out the window.

Alex's smile faltered and she turned again to look out. Avoiding his gaze, she didn't want to let him know how he affected her. 'It's so perfectly uniform. It reminds me of the little alpine villages in Austria.' She couldn't stop talking. 'Wait! Are those dog sleds? We have dog sledding here too?'

When Alex braved eye contact again, she saw that he was smiling broadly at her. 'We do.'

'That's fantastic. I've never tried that,' said Alex.

'I could take you if you like,' Bohdi offered.

'Why? Did I bid on that too?'

Bohdi's laughter rang through her headset. It was a sound that she thought could no longer touch her. She was wrong. The sincere rumble of laughter, not the one where he thinks he's funny, but the one where Bohdi has been truly amused, sent a familiar rush of pleasure through her. She couldn't hold back her own smile.

'Too soon?'

Bohdi held up his hand, chuckling, 'No, after last night it's a fair question. And, Alex, I'm sorry for how things transpired, but I have to say, I'm glad you're here.'

'Well, who doesn't like being up above the clouds?' she answered. She tried to keep her tone casual.

Alex watched Bohdi as he looked out the window. He was working his jaw, as though he had something to say, but wasn't sure where to begin. She didn't wait long.

He turned to her. 'Listen, Alex, maybe, I don't know,' he hesitated before continuing. 'Maybe if we could start over. Like we were meeting for the first time. Like we did on the road.'

'On the road?' Alex didn't know where Bohdi was going with this.

'Yeah, well, okay, not quite like that. But maybe as friends. Start over as friends.'

Alex had no idea how to respond. Friends? How could she be a friend to Bohdi? Her whole life, as far back as she could remember, Alex had either loved Bohdi with all her heart or hated him completely.

He had been the only one she had ever wanted. Even in the first few years after Ben's death, she had still dreamed of him at night, when she hadn't yet learned to control her thoughts. She had pictured a life together, marriage, blue-eyed babies, and growing old. But that is what children do, and when little girls grow up, they learn to know the difference between fantasy and reality. Bohdi Vonn was a fantasy… a gorgeous, fun fantasy. But the reality was, he was reckless. Reckless with people's lives, and reckless with their hearts. She didn't need that in her life, and she needed to remember that.

So, then why was she considering his offer of peace? She was going to be gone in a few short days. Maybe he was right. Perhaps for the few days here she could, not forget, but maybe push aside the anger and hostility.

Compartmentalize… she was good at that. Why make this any harder than it needed to be? Enjoy a few moments and then move on, leaving Talisman and Bohdi Vonn behind her, forever. Isn't that what she really came here to do?

'Alright.'

'Alright?' He looked so relieved that she wanted to laugh.

'Yes, alright. We can start over. Not like on the road, but as two people simply enjoying an incredible experience together.' Alex hoped she was clear.

'Okay, let's do it. We are starting over.'

Bohdi already had that familiar twinkle in his eyes. 'So… you single?'

'Really? This is where you're starting?' Alex shook her head. The man was incorrigible.

'Yes, really. That's a fair question. It's certainly one I ask all the ladies I meet.'

'You didn't ask me that out on the road.'

'The road? I've only just met you now. Listen, Alex, if we are going to do this, I'm going to need you to focus.' Bohdi's look of admonishment was comical.

'You believe I would have come looking for you at the T-Bar if I had someone else in my life?'

Bohdi shrugged. 'Some women do.'

'Well, I take offense to that. I would think you would know me better—'

'Isn't that the point? I hardly know you at all. Are you some billionaire's bored wife, looking for some fun in the mountains? I don't know.'

Alex rolled her eyes. 'Are you finished? Moving on…'

'Don't think I missed that you still haven't answered the question, Alex.'

'Which one? Am I a bored wife?'

'Are you single?' he asked again.

Alex laughed. This was so much easier. Yes, compartmentalize and pretend. She could deal with reality later.

'Yes, Bohdi, shockingly enough, I am, in fact, single.' For a moment she could have sworn she heard him mutter 'good' into the headset, but his face reflected nothing. 'What? Does that surprise you?'

Bohdi gave her an exaggerated once-over. 'Actually, yes it does. Someone like you, beautiful, smart, successful, confident, athletic, beautiful—'

'You already said that.'

'I'm making my point.'

Alex ignored his flattery. 'I would ask you the same, but I think I've already gathered the answer.'

'What is that supposed to mean?'

'Single, not lonely. I didn't miss all the broken hearts as a result of Jaz's misguided scheme. I almost feel guilty for taking you away from all your admirers and preventing you from a chance to find 'the one'.'

'Really, you think that love can be bought in a silent auction?'

'I'm not sure. I would have to run the numbers on similar scenarios. Anything else would be an assumption.'

'You need to run the numbers? You're a funny girl, Alex Mason.'

'Beautiful too, or at least I've been told. Multiple times,' she gave Bohdi a wink. 'Hmm… really, why am I single?'

'You're forgetting modest,' accused Bohdi.

Alex smiled as she replied, 'I wasn't forgetting. I was leaving that one for you.'

'Ouch.'

She waved away his feigned hurt. 'Please, you put yourself up as a prize in a charitable auction.'

'Maybe I'm worth it.'

Alex gave him a questionable look. 'How much did I pay for you again?'

'You don't want to know.'

'In that case you're lucky I believe in the cause.'

Bohdi grinned. 'I'm lucky you're rich.'

A crackle came through the headsets as their pilot cleared his throat and spoke.

'You folks ready to touch down?'

Alex had forgotten about their pilot. She looked over at Bohdi. He gave her a smile and nodded.

Alex nodded back. 'Sounds good.'

***

The helicopter brought them to an open expanse of snow that looked like a smear of smooth icing between a collection of jagged peaks. They landed and stepped out, instantly sinking into the deep powder. Bohdi unloaded their gear. He'd spent time as a guide for this tour many times, so he waved off their pilot, knowing where they would meet him at the bottom. As the chopper lifted off, he wrapped his arms around Alex, protecting her from the spray.

He could see her eyebrows lift behind her goggles. He shrugged and yelled, 'Hard to shake my white knight role.'

Alex tapped her helmet and shook her head.

'Never mind, I just wanted to have the chance to hold you.'

Alex shook her head again, but this time gave a thumbs up. Bohdi was pretty sure she hadn't heard a word.

Once the helicopter flew off, they quickly sorted out their gear and put their equipment on. They stood together in a reverential moment of silence as they took in the panorama around them.

'I don't think we could have gotten a better day for this,' said Bohdi. 'Bluebird skies and waist-deep champagne powder!'

'I cannot believe this view,' replied Alex. 'Seriously, it's incredible!'

It sure was. The look of pure joy on her face hit him hard in the chest. How could a simple thing like a smile have such an effect? He didn't want to screw this up. He needed to stay focused on the mountain.

'I gotta tell you, Alex. There is nothing like standing atop an unnamed peak, looking at a slope rollover so steep that it drops out of sight.'

Alex sidled over a little closer to him, a sharp line between her brows. 'I thought we were starting out with an easier run?'

Bohdi quickly reassured her, 'We are. It only looks that way from here. In 20 metres you'll be cutting tracks on smooth, unbroken powder. No pillow lines, no problems. Only sunshine and untouched terrain. Besides, it's all what's called Hero Snow, so you can't go wrong.'

'I know what it's called. Give me a moment.'

Bohdi waited, silently, until he saw her exhale and square her shoulders. He gently checked her hip. 'You good?'

Alex gave him a half-smile and nodded. 'Good.' She moved closer to the edge of the run then hesitated.

He wondered if he should say more to put her at ease, but he didn't want to belabour the point. She would be fine. She never stopped skiing. She only stopped skiing at Talisman.

'Ready to rip?' he shouted. Alex didn't turn around, but she gave him two thumbs up. Bohdi moved up, coming behind Alex, his skis on either side of hers. Alex froze, and for a moment she relaxed back into his body.

'You got this,' he said.

Alex only nodded in response, then broke forward. She was slow at first, like she was feeling out her legs, and then Bohdi caught the moment that she remembered what to do.

Alex was a graceful skier. And like her brother had been, she was fast. Really fast. Bohdi had been following behind, making sure she was comfortable on the run. But as her confidence on skis returned, Bohdi could feel his own speed picking up. They weren't racing each other, but it began to feel like an elaborate game of cat and mouse. As Bohdi followed Alex's lead, a strange excitement was building inside of him, with no relation to the mountain at all. The feeling didn't leave him all morning.

Usually there would be a guaranteed seven runs for a heli-ski trip, but with the side tour they had taken, Bohdi and Alex were only able to fit three in before stopping for their packed lunch. They were both starving when the helicopter touched down to grab them at the bottom of their third run.

Bohdi quickly conversed with the pilot, agreeing on a location for lunch. Paul took them up to the top of a wide-open glacier, with wicked chutes that ran along the side. The men both knew it was one of the best views from the mountain and they wanted Alex to see it firsthand.

Sandwich in hand, Alex pointed to the chutes. 'This is unbelievable, but you guys don't honestly intend to take me over there, do you?'

Paul chuckled, 'I'll take you wherever you want to go, but I can't say I recommend it. Bohdi here has spent some time over there though.'

'Don't worry, I have no interest in weaving through those rock bands again,' said Bohdi. 'That was business, not pleasure. Well, maybe a little pleasure,' he confessed.

'Business?' asked Alex.

'That particular spot was for a Warren Miller film. Needed a big backdrop. But usually it was other locations.'

‘Movies? I didn’t know you were acting.’ Alex looked confused.

‘Mostly stunt work, you know, the name in scrolling credits that no one notices.’ Bohdi narrowed his gaze at Alex.

She didn’t look impressed. ‘Sounds reckless.’

Her casual reply felt like an accusation and Bohdi didn’t like it. ‘Definitely not. There is more stable snowpack on those steep faces. That’s why you can bag big lines. Anywhere else would be unsafe. I’m not reckless, Alex, not anymore.’

She studied him then shrugged. ‘Fine, I just hadn’t realized you were in the movies.’

‘I hadn’t realized you’ve been following my career.’

Alex looked upward and then back to Bohdi. ‘The whole world followed you. It was hard to miss you.’

Bohdi noticed that once again she had avoided answering his question. Alex Mason was an expert at avoiding the uncomfortable, but this wasn’t the time to push.

She smiled over to Paul. ‘I’m happy with backcountry and bottomless powder. I’ll let Bohdi tackle the steeps.’

Bohdi jumped back to his feet. ‘Why don’t we head out then? I want to be sure you’re getting your money’s worth.’

He knew he sounded sour, and so did Alex when she grabbed his hand and pulled him back down on the snow beside her. ‘That’s true. You’re on my time today, so relax, Bohdi. Drink it in. You need to sit still and enjoy the moment.’

She didn’t even blink as she said it and he wasn’t going to argue by pointing out her hypocrisy. He was not going to be the one to break their fledgling truce. He also didn’t mind spending a little more time sitting on top of the world, with an interesting and beautiful woman. Maybe she would start talking, and if Bohdi was going to ever figure out Alex Mason, he had better start taking notes.

CHAPTER TEN

Bohdi was still ahead of her, but only by a few ski lengths. Alex was hot on his heels. Her legs were burning, but she was not giving up. When Bohdi announced their last run of the day, it was Alex who had challenged him to a race. His hesitation surprised her, but Alex threw enough insults at his ego, he eventually capitulated. But now he was winning, and her competitive streak was coming alive.

Whipping through the spray of her own powder, Alex could taste the sweet, fresh mountain air with every ragged breath. It was better than she remembered. Her heart was thumping against her chest in exertion and exhilaration. She had no intention of losing this race to Mr. Olympics, but there was no denying his smooth skill from her vantage point.

She was following his tracks, and each twist and turn he took she matched, her hips mimicking the motions of his, like a seductive dance on the snow. They were in perfect rhythm, and while she moved in time with him, the fire in her legs moved up to settle between her thighs.

Their bodies weren't even touching, and hers was reacting like she was entwined in some mesmerizing, seductive dance with Bohdi. Alex had spent time with a Spanish dance instructor who was determined to teach her the Bachata and that had never felt this sensual. What was this hold that Bohdi had over her? Even now, years after she had rid her heart of him.

The heated distraction of her body and mind had allowed Bohdi to increase his lead. Alex was about to tuck in and catch up when Bohdi's left ski flew out and he began a mad tumble down in a show of flailing legs and arms. When he came to a halt, he was spread out on his back and didn't move.

'Bohdi!'

Frantic, Alex rushed to his side, a waterfall of snow inadvertently spraying Bohdi as she abruptly stopped beside him.

'Bohdi?'

Alex popped off her skis and knelt down, ripping off her gloves, lifting his goggles, and wiping the wet snow from his face. His eyes opened.

'Are you alright?' Alex was still brushing snow from his cheeks with her thumbs.

Bohdi shook out his legs and arms. 'I'm good. But my ego may be badly bruised.'

Alex sat back in the deep powder, pulled off her helmet, and threw an additional handful of snow at him.

'Seriously, Bohdi. You scared me.'

He put both arms up in defense. 'You realize this wasn't planned?'

'I can never tell with you.'

'Ouch. I told you my ego was bruised… no need to add to the injury.'

His wounded look did nothing to deter her.

'You realize this makes me the winner?' Alex looked down at him with a cocky smile.

Bohdi sat up, looking past her up the hill at his ski, then back to her. Alex glanced to Bohdi's lost ski, then met his blue gaze. The glint in his eye wasn't enough warning for her to stop him. Bohdi grinned as he grabbed one of her skis and threw it up the hill.

'Cheater!' cried Alex and she scrambled up the hill towards her ski. She almost had it, when Bohdi grabbed her boot from behind, dragging her back down towards him. She tried to kick him off, but in seconds, he flipped her over and was sitting over her, knees on either side of her hips. Bohdi leaned forward, his hands on either side of her head.

'I'm afraid I can't let you get that ski, Alex.' His voice was low and husky.

Alex's pulse quickened and the warmth she had felt earlier spread throughout her body in a ripple of tingles. The nearness of him was taking her breath away faster than the high altitude.

'Why not?' she breathed.

'Because I really hate to lose.'

'So do I.'

'Then we're at an impasse. What are you going to do about it?' he asked.

Alex closed her eyes. Nothing made sense. How far was she going to let this go? She opened them again to see those blue eyes peering into her soul, asking her for something she wasn't sure she could give, even if she wanted to. And right now, she really wanted to.

'Doesn't your wipe-out automatically grant me the win?' Her voice wavered as she spoke.

'That's how you want to win?'

'Yes.' Alex wasn't sure she was talking about their race anymore. Bohdi smelled of sunshine and heat. She was sure the intensity between them was quantifiable.

'Do you always get your way?'

'Yes,' replied Alex.

'Then I guess you're the winner.' His head dropped down, his mouth moments from hers. Alex could feel the warmth of his breath on her face.

She remained still, frozen to the snow, unsure if she should break the spell he was weaving, when his lips brushed against her ear. 'Are you sure you can handle the prize?'

Closing her eyes, Alex inhaled sharply and whispered, 'Yes.'

He tilted her head and kissed her softly on the side of her neck. Alex gasped. His gentle touch was unexpected. It was like he had taken all the air from her lungs without even touching her mouth. The heat of his lips worked their way along her jawline until Bohdi's mouth caught hers. Alex brought her hands to his head and she pulled off his helmet, releasing the last of his restraint.

His lips crashed into hers, desperate and needing. Alex moaned, and her body rose against him in response. She found her lips parting, seeking the warmth of his mouth. They were on top of a snow-covered world, but it all fell away. There was no past, no future, only this moment engulfing her completely.

'Alex,' he groaned as he captured her lips once again. She could barely hear him over the pounding of her heart.

It was supposed to be just a kiss, but it wasn't. After all this time, it was everything and it was too much.

Alex pulled back. 'Bohdi… I'

Bohdi paused, his eyes searching hers, needing an explanation, but she couldn't grant him one. He leaned forward, touching his forehead to hers, his eyes closed.

For a moment, they lay there, frozen breath joining in the fragile space between them. It was Bohdi who broke the silence.

'Okay… okay.'

His low murmur sent another shiver through Alex.

'Okay,' she whispered back.

He lifted himself from her body and flopped back onto the snow beside her, both of them staring in silence up to a cloudless sky.

Alex wasn't sure what to say. What was there to say? That the kiss she had shared with Bohdi set off an explosion of need and craving. That it awakened something she had hoped to bury forever. That the confusion swirling around her head was fighting with her desire to roll over and kiss him again. No, there was only one thing to do. Ignore the lingering heat still on her lips and pretend it never happened. In order for that plan to work she needed Bohdi to pretend too.

Alex cleared her throat. 'We should be moving. Our ride is expecting us.'

'Of course.' Bohdi stood up. 'We should go.'

He extended his hand to help her up, pulled his helmet back on, and then climbed up to grab his wayward ski. Alex did the same.

When they both clicked in their bindings, Bohdi shouted over, 'Good?'

Good? No, Alex was far from good. Her thoughts were a chaotic mess of craving and confusion. Her body was another matter completely. It had finally tasted Bohdi Vonn and it was hungry for more. Alex was losing the control she had spent so long cultivating.

Bohdi tilted his head again in question. Alex gave him thumbs up.

'Yeah, all good.'

***

His whole body was shaking. Bohdi was sure Alex could tell how unsettled he was when it took him three attempts to get his boots back in his bindings. He wanted to say something, anything, about what had happened, but he didn't want to scare Alex with the intensity of his desire.

Pretend it didn't happen, that's what she wanted to do. But Bohdi couldn't do the same. Not forever anyway. He wasn't built like that. He would let Alex have her way, for now. Get to the bottom of the run, and maybe then they could talk. He needed to give her some time. Unfortunately, that was the one thing they were short on. He didn't have the luxury of stepping back and seeing where things might take them. He could try and ignore the fierce attraction between them, but with RG Holdings arriving tomorrow, Bohdi knew that he was running out of time to convince Alex that selling the resort would be a mistake.

She dropped into the wide bowl, ripping fresh lines as she carved through the snow. Alex might claim not to remember the fun they had as kids on the hill, but her legs sure did. She looked like a powder hound who had been skiing the backcountry her whole life.

He couldn't understand why she was so eager to give up something that brought her joy. Despite her determination to erase Talisman from her memory, Alex's mood lightened with every run. The fresh air brightened her cheeks, matching the excitement that radiated from her eyes. He didn't see the sadness that always lurked around the edges of their conversations. She wasn't just on the mountain; the mountain was still inside of her. He was sure of it.

They made short work of the rest of the run, stopping only briefly when they needed to catch their breath or to admire another incredible view.

The helicopter was waiting for them when they arrived at the meet zone and, other than sharing her excitement of the day with Paul, Alex made no reference to what had happened between them. Bohdi was starting to wonder how far she would take this. How long could she sidestep the truth?

Bohdi held out his hand to assist Alex into the helicopter; she hesitated then took the help. Her hand fit perfectly in his. He waited an extra moment before he let go. He doubted Alex would let him hold it for the entire ride.

When Bohdi organized the second half of the auction prize package, he had no idea that it would be Alex accompanying him. Given their shared moment earlier he wasn't sure now how receptive Alex would be to the rest of his plans. He looked over to see if she had noticed that they weren't flying directly back to the resort.

The fading sun outside the window was highlighting her profile, and the corners of Bohdi's mouth lifted as he watched contentment cross her face. It was the expression he was hoping to see, that moment in time when you realize you're staring at something special. Alex was gazing at it outside her window, but Bohdi knew it was seated next to him in a bright pink jacket.

He didn't say a word. He wanted Alex to soak it in, feel the call of the mountain, and remember where she was from. Who she could still be, if she wanted it. The question was what did Alex want?

'You guys want to see more, or get to the lodge?' The pilot's voice crackled through the headsets.

'Lodge is good. Thanks, Paul,' replied Bohdi.

'Lodge?'

Alex turned her attention from the window, her eyes fixed on him.

'Well, after a day like this you don't finish up with beer and nachos. Kinda takes away from the magic.'

Alex looked out the window and then back to him. 'So where exactly is this lodge?'

Leaning over her, Bohdi pointed out the window. 'Over there. We are still a few minutes out.'

'Where? I don't see it,' said Alex.

'You're looking down. You need to look up.'

Bohdi pointed again, and this time Alex saw it. She took in a sharp breath.

'Oh wow,' she exhaled.

Neither of them said a word, as they approached the mountainside building.

The Vista Lodge was designed with indulgence in mind. Its exterior echoed the traditional alpine style of the resort below. The enormous windows allowed nearly every room to take in the sweeping views across the valley. It was a perfect way to end the day in high altitude decadence.

The helicopter dropped down to land on the dedicated helipad and Bohdi and Alex proceeded into the stone and timber-framed lodge. They were welcomed by the staff and brought into a gorgeous triple-height great room with a roaring log fire. As Bohdi and Alex settled in, the staff disappeared.

'Well,' said Alex. 'This is truly something.'

Bohdi looked around. 'Sure is. I haven't been here in a long time. It's usually reserved by guests looking to take their experience to greater heights.'

'Funny guy.' Alex closed her eyes and shook her head at his terrible pun. 'I imagine some might find this rather romantic. Now I'm feeling really guilty for taking this away from some unlucky girl. Her chance to spend time here with the famous Bohdi Vonn ruined by dirty gameplay.'

'Then I hope you'll appreciate it all the more.' He ignored the shot she sent his direction on the nefarious way she had arrived here. 'You're right, it is pretty romantic up here.'

Was Alex trying to tell him something? Why would she have made a comment like that? Who knows what she was thinking? She was definitely wrong about one thing though.

'You know, you're overstating the whole famous thing. In a few more years no one will remember my name. I'll simply be a guy who made it to the Olympics but could never bring home gold. I got lucky with the endorsements and film work. But I leave behind no legacy, Alex. And I'm fine with it. The truth is I can't wait to be just another face.'

'I don't know if I buy that.'

Bohdi couldn't be sure which part of his confession she was dismissing, but she kept talking so he didn't interrupt.

'But I certainly can't deny that I am getting my money's worth. Award-winning chef, indoor pool, and a fully equipped gym. I'm assuming the linens are of the finest quality?' She smoothed the leather of the couch with her palm as she spoke. 'Are we actually making money on this?'

'Not my place and I'm not the numbers guy. Weren't you looking into all of that?'

'I was going to, today, but someone decided to foil my plans,' she replied.

'Hey, remember, it wasn't me,' Bohdi protested.

'You, your people, I consider you all responsible, but,' she conceded, 'maybe this isn't all bad. And of course, a good cause.'

'I'm going to take that as absolution.'

'Of course you will.'

It was rewarding to see the smile on her face reach her eyes, and it warmed him to know he was capable of putting it there. Alex shivered and Bohdi stood up, wincing as he walked over to poke the fire.

'Feet hurt? Boots a little tight?'

Bohdi wiggled his right foot. 'No, I must have stubbed my toe last night. It's still a little sore.' The flames kicked up as he stoked the fire. Bohdi twirled the poker in his hand. He needed to talk to her about the sale. He was running out of time, but he didn't want to create any further tension between them. He knew this peace between them was tenuous at best.

'You had fun today?'

Alex hesitated and her eyes narrowed as she stared at him. 'Yes, but…' she faltered. 'Yes, the skiing was excellent. You were right; I'm glad I had the chance to see it all. It was good that I went. And this,' Alex indicated her surroundings. ‘Well, this isn’t too shabby either. A girl can’t complain about all of this, that’s for sure.’

Bohdi knew he had to ask the question. ‘Then what do you think?’

Alex scrunched up her face. ‘What do you mean, what do I think?’

‘I mean, what do you think about keeping Talisman, about holding off on the sale—’

‘Whoa, whoa, Bohdi,’ Alex held up her palms. ‘Stop, please.’

‘I’m just saying, you saw for yourself how special this place is. Why throw that away?’

Tilting her head, she squinted at him. ‘What did you think? That I would spend the day skiing with you and change my mind? Distracted by snowy landscapes and warm log fires? That spectacular views and luxurious surroundings would make me forget what needed to be done? My father is gone, Bohdi. My family is no longer a part of this place.’

Bohdi moved to sit next to her on the large couch and Alex placed a pillow between them.

‘That’s not true. Your family is this place. I won’t ask you to stay, Alex, but don’t sell. Not to RG Holdings. Let Cal run the place. I can help him.’

‘Cal? Have you seen him recently? The man is done. Probably been done with Talisman for a while. And you? I don’t think so, Bohdi. You don’t get to have it all.’

‘Have it all? What are you even talking about,’ demanded Bohdi.

Alex sighed, ‘Nothing. I don’t know why we are talking about this again. I thought we were going to enjoy this day. Can’t you drop it?’

Bohdi didn’t want to drop it. Alex didn’t get to make all the rules. He didn’t understand why she was so adamant that selling was her only option. He wasn’t asking her to stay. He couldn’t, despite the deep desire of his heart. Hell, he wanted her to go, needed her to leave. He wouldn't be able to handle seeing Alex Mason everyday anyway. She was a reminder of one more thing he could never have.

The sound of a cleared throat announced their butler, inviting them into the dining room for dinner.

Bohdi looked over to Alex, who raised her brow and pleaded, 'Can we please stop talking about this? Enjoy our dinner?'

'Fine,' he growled, turning his back on Alex as he stomped into the dining room.

CHAPTER ELEVEN

Alex stood, watching as Bohdi stormed off. She hadn't intended to get him so riled up. He was taking this all so personally. He sure wasn't holding up his end of the bargain. They were supposed to go skiing, see the resort. It should have been one uncomplicated, simple day, avoiding all uncomfortable conversation. But Bohdi couldn't help himself… he needed to control and fix what wasn't even a problem. Why didn't he realize that it wasn't his problem and nothing would change for him? That it was better for both of them if she sold the resort and they never saw each other again. Especially after what happened between them.

He wasn't completely wrong. She had been affected by her surroundings. Today had relit a spark in her and it surprised her. It was being out on the mountain, reconnecting with nature. It resonated with a part of her she had spent years trying to suppress. Weekend ski trips and holidays never filled her the way Talisman did.

And then there had been that kiss. That unexpected and devastating kiss. It lit more than a spark. The explosion between them started a fire and Alex knew if she didn't leave soon, she would only get burned.

Thinking of it now was sending a ripple of heat through her that even the roaring fire in the room could not explain. The moment that his warm mouth touched her neck, all of

Alex's defenses were gone, and she knew she was helpless. It wasn't simple lust. It was relief, it was need, and it was frightening.

Alex shook the dangerous imagery from her mind and straightened her shoulders. She could handle this. There was no point in entertaining any other notion. She was more than capable of pushing aside thoughts that were better disregarded. Bohdi was going to have to move on, just like her. An incredible meal was waiting and right now she was ravenous.

He was waiting for her at the end of the long mahogany dining table, his arms crossed tightly over his chest. He gave her a forced smile as she sat down.

'Looks wonderful,' she said.

Bohdi didn't answer. His lips were still clenched together. Alex wasn't sure if he was angry or pouting; either way she didn't think he would appreciate it if she laughed at him. There was something amusing about a frustrated Bohdi. He was so awful at hiding it Alex assumed he usually got his way. Well, Bohdi Vonn wasn't used to dealing with her.

'You're not hungry?' Alex waved her fork in the direction of his plate. 'I'm starving.'

'Then you should eat.'

He was sulking. Alex didn't even try to hide the half smile that touched her lips.

'I will, thank you.'

Bohdi must be famished. Their day had guaranteed an appetite. Was he trying to prove a point by refusing to eat? It was a waste of his time. She was not going to talk about the sale. If he wanted to act like a child, then she would treat him like one. A distraction was in order.

'When did you come back to Talisman?'

He looked at her in open surprise. 'When did I…' Bohdi threw up his hands. 'Fine, fine. When did I come back? Almost two years ago. That what you're looking for?'

'Why did you come back, why here?'

Bohdi now looked confused by her questions, which was better than his anger. Alex realized that it wasn't only for distraction that she asked. She really wanted to know. Why had he come back here? He had travelled all over the globe… why had he chosen to relocate here? What did he hope to gain?

He picked up his cutlery and began to eat while he studied her. Alex waited until he was ready to respond. He was rolling the fork over in his fingers, as if he wasn't sure she would like his answer.

'It was Jim. Your dad is the reason I'm here.'

If he was looking to shock her, he succeeded.

'My father? What did he have to do with it? He never even told me you were back. Why?'

'Why didn't he tell you or why did he invite me back?'

'Both.'

'I can't answer the first question for you—'

'Fine. What did you mean, he was the reason you came back?' she demanded.

Bohdi drew in a long breath as he stared across the table at her. Why was he hesitating? It wasn't a difficult question.

'I was here for a movie. My knee was healed enough that I could work again. Another Olympics was out. I had no chance at gold, maybe I never did. Either way, I couldn't train at the same level anymore. So, I took a job that happened to be filming here. I didn't know where it would be when I signed the contract, but that's how it turned out.'

He lifted his shoulder in a half shrug and then continued, 'Your dad and I started talking one night and the idea of the T-Bar came up.'

'Hold on. He hasn't seen you in years and suddenly you're building a pub together?' What was Bohdi talking about? It made absolutely no sense. Out of the blue he decided to forgive and go into business with Bohdi. What was she missing? What wasn't he telling her?

'What do you mean in years? I never stopped talking to your dad. We've... he's always been there. We never stopped speaking to each other, Alex. He's always been a part of my life.'

'He never said anything to me!'

'Why would he?' Bohdi asked.

'How about because I'm his daughter, because you... you...' Alex paused. 'Because he should have. That's why.'

Bohdi shrugged again. 'Again, I can't answer that for you. All I can say is that Jim, your dad... he was a good man.'

'So, what happened, why did you open the T-Bar?'

'I was done. I was tired, and Jim could see it. I'd been running, moving, constantly in motion since... well, for a long time anyway. He knew it and so he offered me another option. An opportunity to come back to a place that could fill the hollow—' Bohdi stopped. He was looking at her with glistening eyes. 'Let's say he gave me a second chance. For that I will always be grateful.'

Bohdi looked back down to his plate. 'I miss him.'

It was obvious he was sincere. Not even Bohdi was that good of an actor. His grief was etched into the lines of his face. She didn't want to ask the question, but her guilt drove her words. 'Was he lonely? Did he ever... did he ever have anyone?'

'He had everyone.'

Alex fought back her tears. She didn't dare speak, knowing any words would be caught in her throat. Everyone? How could he say that? Her father didn't have Ben and he didn't have her. But what could she say? She really didn't know what her father had been thinking. No matter what she or her mother thought about Bohdi, her father carried no grudge towards him. Maybe he was desperate to regain the son he had lost. Alex would never know. She never bothered to take the time to ask. She had been too wrapped up in her own hurt, in her mother's grief. Bohdi may have been responsible for so much of their pain, but he had not run. Alex would give him that. He obviously cared deeply for her father and there was no proof it wasn't returned. It was more than she had done. Decency forced her to acknowledge that.

'Thank you, Bohdi.'

His head whipped up, blue eyes not understanding.

'Thank you for being there for him. I'm sure it meant a lot to him. It does… it does to me.'

He didn't respond. He cleared his throat and nodded.

They didn't speak as they made short work of their dinner. The wild salmon was cooked to perfection and the chocolate indulgence for dessert was a necessary finish. Alex understood why Talisman had won the resort award. The meal alone was worth every penny.

As she willed herself not to lick the last vestiges of chocolate from her plate, she noticed Bohdi was staring at her. He was never down for long. Somewhere through dinner he had lost the sadness that shadowed him, and the spark of mischief was back in his eye. Alex wasn't sure which one was more dangerous to her heart.

'If you've given up on that plate, there is one more part to this package.'

Unapologetic, she swiped a finger through the last hint of chocolate on her plate and licked it clean. 'And what exactly is that?'

Bohdi cleared his throat in response, 'Come with me.'

He led her from the dining room, back to the great room. He stood next to the tall windows and pointed out to a steaming hot tub that met with the edge of the mountain.

'Ohh, lovely, how did I not notice that when we came in?'

'I've often been called distracting.'

'Among other things, I'm sure.'

'Ouch. You're a hard woman, Alex Mason.'

'I have faith you'll recover.'

'At least you still have faith in me.'

'I have faith in your ability to bounce back.'

'Well, if your faith—'

'Okay! Enough. So, this is the piece de resistance? The finale to the day?'

'Can you think of anything better?'

His grin was contagious, and Alex found herself smiling back. It looked inviting, he looked inviting. It was a good thing they weren't going in. It was a delicious recipe for disaster.

'I'm out of luck. You didn't provide an itinerary, so… I didn't pack my bathing suit.'

'You didn't need to.' He lifted one brow in her direction and a tingle of excitement shot through her.

'I'm not skinny-dipping with you, Bohdi.' Alex wasn't sure she meant it, but it still needed to be said.

'You wound me. You're not the only one who can be prepared.'

What did the man have up his sleeve? There was no doubt by that twinkle in his eye that there was something.

'Enlighten me.'

'On the off chance you were inclined, I had Jaz grab a bathing suit from the shop.' Bohdi was practically bouncing on his toes he was so pleased with himself. He was painfully adorable.

'Of course you did. You guys certainly thought of everything.'

'Well, you are paying for the full experience.'

Alex looked back out to the hot tub. Who was she kidding? She wanted to ease her tired body into the steaming water right now. The problem was that she wouldn't be in there alone. Could she still maintain her casual detachment from Bohdi if she did? Her track record today was proving otherwise.

Turning to Bohdi and his hopeful grin, she felt her resolve to maintain distance from him weaken. It had been a long day of hard work. Her body deserved the reward and, after all, this was all part the package she had paid for. Value for money. It only made sense.

'Fine,' she agreed.

'Fine,' said Bohdi as he pointed down the hall. 'The change room and doors out are that way.'

***

Bohdi silently blew the air from his cheeks as he watched Alex make her way across the radiant heat of the stone patio to where he was waiting inside the hot tub. The water was hot, but it was nothing compared to the burn of desire that washed over him as she dropped her robe and stepped down into the sunken pool. He looked out over the mountain so she wouldn't see the craving in his eyes.

He glanced back and cleared his throat. 'It fits?'

Alex gave him a knowing look. 'Barely.'

Bohdi held up his hands, 'Hey! I didn't—'

'I know, I know, it's all Jaz,' Alex interrupted. 'I'll thank her later.'

'Me too,' Bohdi muttered under his breath as Alex gave him a withering stare.

He needed to change topics or he was going to get himself in trouble. He pointed out to the panoramic view of the valley below. 'I don't think you'll find a better view.'

'There have been several of these moments today, for sure. I may have to concede to your knowledge in these matters. This is the perfect way to end a day.'

Bohdi couldn't agree more. Although he wanted to discuss RG Holdings, he also wanted to simply enjoy this moment with Alex. He knew it was fleeting, that there would not be another. He accepted that was how it had to be. Those concerns were for tomorrow. There was still time for pleasure tonight.

The moon over the mountains was creating a perfect winter light. Bohdi was having difficulty choosing between the uninterrupted views of the snow-covered peaks and valleys or the achingly beautiful woman in front of him. He chose the latter.

'You know, this is where I had my first kiss,' he told her.

'Ha! I doubt that,' said Alex. The tinkle of her laughter and the hum of the hot tub were the only other sounds in the tranquil setting.

'It's true. Not here, down there. At the resort.'

'Now that makes more sense. Who was the lucky girl?'

'Lucky? I'm flattered.'

'Well, I could say unfortunate—'

'Never mind that, forget I said it.' Bohdi shook his head with a smile of reproach. 'It was a long time ago, but do you remember that Columbian family?'

'I remember,' said Alex.

'They were the ones with all the bodyguards. Here for a couple weeks making everyone uncomfortable.'

Alex's eyes widened. 'You made out with one of the bodyguards? You were, what, 14?'

Bohdi laughed at the incredulous expression on her face. 'No, no. The daughter! I kissed the daughter.'

'You seriously thought that kissing the daughter of the head of some cartel was a good idea?'

'No, no. He was a money laundering guy or something. At least I think he was. I don't actually know.'

Alex wasn't impressed. 'You really are reckless. Do you even know what could have happened if you were caught?'

'Oh, I think Eva had plenty of practice evading her father's watchful eyes.'

Bohdi was smiling at the memory when Alex asked, 'Do you know if… who Ben's was?'

'Yup.'

'Who?'

'Eva.' His bark of laughter rolled over the side of the mountain.

'What? You're joking.' Alex splashed a palm of water in his direction. 'The same girl?'

'Oh yeah. Same time. Well, she kissed Ben first.'

Alex rolled her eyes. 'That's disgusting.'

'That's 14. We had never seen anything like her. She was so exotic and so… 16. I think she liked the complete control she held over us. We would have done anything for her.'

'Well, I guess I should say good for her.'

'Good for her? Sure. Devastating for us when she left.'

Alex was quiet for a moment then spoke. 'Ben loved it here.'

Bohdi inhaled sharply. She had said it softly, almost a whisper. Did she even mean to say it aloud? He didn't think he would ever be talking about Ben with Alex. He responded carefully, worried he was walking on a field of land mines.

'He really did. He loved it all.' Bohdi waited, and when Alex didn't speak, he continued. 'I think he tore through every bit of rideable terrain. Ben was always itching to push the envelope further. When I met him, I knew instantly we were going to be friends.'

Alex didn't respond as she swirled her hands in the water in front of her. She lifted them out, wiping them across the scented towels on the edge and turned around to rest her chin on her arms, gazing out. Bohdi moved through the water to join her at the edge of the tub. When his elbow brushed against her arm, she stiffened and then relaxed.

'I wish… Ben would have liked this place, this lodge.' Alex briefly closed her eyes, her mouth curving into a small smile as she gave her head a shake. 'Although, between the two of you, I'm sure it would have been turned into a chalet of ill repute. I don't think the Resort Awards would have been as forthcoming.'

'Probably right.'

He didn't need to say anymore. He wasn't sure if Alex was too far off the mark. He often wondered the same things. What would life have been like if Ben had survived the accident? He had no doubt they would still be friends, but would they have matured over time? It was almost impossible to imagine the ones you have lost as anything other than as they were. Ben would always be young and carefree, but his loss ensured that his sister was not.

Warming her shoulders against the frosty air, Alex dipped them below the water level then back up again. Bohdi was envious of the water caressing every inch of her skin.

'It still hurts, Bohdi. Sometimes you live with the pain for so long you can forget that it's there. But it's not gone, it's never gone.'

Alex didn't look at him while she spoke. Bohdi didn't want her to. He wasn't sure he could handle seeing the pain in her eyes, a pain that he could have prevented if he had been a little faster or that much stronger. He knew exactly what Alex was talking about. He lived with it everyday. For years it haunted his dreams.

'I'm so sorry. Alex.'

She ignored his apology and said, 'I don't understand how my father was able to stay here. How it was so easy to accept what happened.'

Bohdi drew back from Alex, gently turning her shoulder, forcing her to face him.

'Easy? I don't think it was easy for him at all. I think it was his love for Ben that kept him here. It's what made him still feel connected to his son. I think the only thing he accepted was that time moved forward whether he wanted it to or not. He was dedicated to helping others, like the Para Alpine program and keeping Talisman the jewel that it was, the place Ben loved.'

Alex searched his face as though seeking for hidden meaning. She wouldn't find any. Bohdi meant what he said.

'Maybe. The truth is I think I missed a lot when it came to my father. I was caught up in my own grief and then my own life. I put up a wall when it came to this place. My father, out of respect to me, never tried to breach it.'

'I'm sure—'

'No, you don't need to make me feel better about it. Did you know that I didn't even know he was gone until after his funeral? His wishes. He didn't want me to feel pressured to come back.' Her lower lip trembled as she continued, 'How selfish was I?'

Bohdi didn't know what to say. Before she arrived, that's exactly how he would have described her. How he had described her. He had no idea that she wasn't even aware of the funeral. It didn't matter. Despite whatever guilt she may have, one thing was true.

'You loved him and he loved you.'

'I know he did.'

'He talked about you all the time.'

She gave a little laugh. 'Well, he forgot to mention you.'

'I'm not totally sure it was because he forgot.'

Alex let out a burst of laughter, but she quickly contained it, as if she were concerned it could turn to tears. Her command over her emotions would have been inspiring if it wasn't so sad. As a child he remembered Alex being a whirling ball of energy and emotion. If she felt it, she said it. No holding back. Did she ever let go anymore?

'It's okay to let it out, Alex.'

She stared at him like he had grown a second nose. 'Let it out? You ever wonder why I went into finance? Numbers, not feelings. So much easier. The emotional needs of relationships are not my thing. It's not that I don't care, Bohdi. I don't want to get hurt. Besides, I'm too busy to get caught up in all of that.'

'Sounds great. You must be a fun first date,' he replied. Then he shook his finger at her. 'You get two hours of my time, but don't get too attached because there won't be a second…' his falsetto cracked on the last word.

Alex narrowed her eyes at his mockery. 'At least I understand that not everything is a joke.'

'What does that mean?'

'It means you're afraid of being serious.'

'Well you're afraid of giving up this façade of control you hold on to. You think you can control everything, but you can't. And I can be serious.'

'I doubt that.'

Something in her words challenged him. The current between them was vibrating and the heat was from more than the hot tub.

Bohdi snaked out an arm and easily pulled her onto his lap. 'Is this serious enough for you?'

Her legs wrapped around his waist and her body trembled in his arms. But Alex's face was expressionless when she answered, lifting her chin. 'You haven't proven anything yet.'

She was definitely challenging him, and it sent his pulse racing.

He ran his fingers along the curve of her spine, coming to rest under the back of her bikini top. He rubbed the soft skin below the clasp, feeling the muscles of her legs twitch in response to the promise of his touch.

'Is this you, telling me that you want me to continue?' With his other hand, Bohdi reached up to hold the back of her neck in his palm, as he leaned forward to whisper in her ear. 'Are you telling me that you want me to kiss you?'

As he spoke, his lips touched the lobe of her ear. Her shudder sent a shiver through him.

'I thought you wanted me to give up control.'

The warmth of her breath on his neck contrasted with the night air. He was sure she could feel his body move in response.

'I do.'

***

Hungry lips crushed hers. Alex opened her mouth and he took her breath, stealing the air from her lungs. This was not like before… this time she could feel his body, touch his skin. The lean torso of the boy she once loved was now filled out with the raw strength of a man. Her fingers danced across the rippling muscles of his back, and she pushed her chest closer to him, desperate for them to meld together as one. Their kiss deepened and time stood still. Nothing else mattered. Only this moment. All she could feel were his hands on her skin and his heart beating against her chest. His uneven breath matched her own, neither willing to give up the other's lips.

She couldn't think, only feel. Every touch of his fingers blazed a burning trail over her skin. The flicking warmth of his tongue creating explosions in her mouth, as his insistent lips conquered hers. Bohdi had taken control of her senses. Her whole body was tingling, and she was becoming weak with need.

His lips broke from hers and she whimpered, the loss of his touch almost too much to bear. Then Bohdi's mouth was on her neck, kissing a line to her ear, gently sucking on the bottom of her lobe. Hot breath as he whispered her name, 'Alexandra.'

Her legs tightened around Bohdi's waist and Alex moaned while she raked her fingers through the soft, wet curls of his dark blonde hair. She wanted more of him, she needed more of him. His greedy lips recaptured hers, swallowing her groans of pleasure.

When she felt the clasp of her bathing suit open to the snap of Bohdi's fingers and the warmth of the water against her bare chest, her eyes snapped open. She pulled back, Bohdi's eyes now open, questioning, not understanding.

It was enough to cause her to pause, to catch a breath, to think. She needed a moment. This was too much, and she was in too deep. If they continued, she would never be able to pretend this didn't mean anything. Not even she could suppress that kind of breach of her senses. She had been wrong to believe she could push aside reality for one day. It was a terrible mistake and if this went any further, Alex didn't know she could fix it.

'Bohdi, I…' she faltered. What could she say?

He lifted his hand to touch her cheek, but she caught it with her hand and brought it down beneath the water.

'Alex, please. Help me unders—'

'I'm sorry, Bohdi, I thought I could. I… you're… I'm sorry. This was a terrible idea. I need to go.' She hastily refastened her bikini top.

She should have known this would happen. That this was the inevitable conclusion of time spent with Bohdi. Alex stepped out of the hot tub and grabbed a nearby towel, leaving Bohdi stunned, still sitting in the water. She didn't look back. She didn't need him to see the tears that rolled down her face.

When she got back to the change room, she sat down on the bench, holding her head in her hands. She looked up to see the mirror in front of her reflecting her misery. She never should have agreed to this lodge. She never should have agreed to go skiing with Bohdi, and she never should have come back to Talisman. Everything had been so clear before she arrived. Sell off her share of Talisman with Cal and move on. This was not the closure she was looking for and now she didn't know what to think.

Alex didn't know how long she could hide in the change room. There wasn't a clock in the room, so she had no idea how much time had passed. It felt like an eternity. It was a relief when she heard the sounds of the helicopter starting up. Bohdi obviously wasn't wasting any time in getting out of here. Alex didn't know if he was furious or confused. He had a right to be both. She wasn't helping anyone with her behavior. She knew there was no point in trying to explain it to Bohdi when she couldn't understand it herself.

She cautiously exited the room. There would be no point in hiding from Bohdi, as she had no other option than to fly back down with him. Alex didn't want to talk about it. He probably felt he was owed an explanation, but she wasn't up for the conversation right now, maybe never. If she were concerned she would be cornered and forced to defend her behavior, she needn't have worried. It was the butler who met her and let her know that her items were already packed and on the helicopter. Bohdi was already onboard.

She thanked him for the stay and made her way out to the helipad. She climbed in and put on her helmet. She glanced over at Bohdi, who gave her a nod. Paul said nothing, giving her a half-hearted smile.

They lifted and swooped down the mountain. There was no further tour or light-hearted banter. It was a straight return back to the resort. Neither the pilot nor Bohdi said a word. It was exactly what she wanted, silence. So why did she feel like she was shattering into a million confused pieces?

CHAPTER TWELVE

Showering after another restless night, Alex let the warm water run over her as she tried to figure out where it all went wrong. It didn't take a genius to realize it was the moment she decided to come back to Talisman and handle the sale herself. Her mother had been right, she should not have returned.

But her mother wasn't right about everything. Talisman wasn't a place that her father loved more than his son. It was a place that he loved because of his son. Alex heard the truth in what Bohdi had said. She was being forced to admit there was something about being back here that reminded her not only of the pain, but of the love Ben had for this place. There were moments yesterday where she could have sworn she heard his whoops of excitement as she swished down a run.

Alex had been too young when Ben died to understand the depths of a father's grief, and too comfortable in her own as the years passed. She finally understood why he had stayed. He didn't want to leave his son behind. How could he? Ben would always be on this mountain. She understood that, but it didn't change things for her. She needed to proceed as planned. What was she going to do? Stay here and avoid Bohdi for the rest of her life? Watch as he moved on, like he always had? Not a chance.

The representatives from the acquisitions department of RG were arriving any minute. She and Cal were going to meet with them and complete this once and for all. She wasn't destroying her father's legacy, no matter what Bohdi implied. She had Cal's assurances that RG was committed to preserving her father's vision. She would confirm that with them herself. Besides, it was an immensely profitable venture; there was no need for change.

Fresh and focused, Alex walked down to Cal's office, refusing to even glance the T-Bar's way. The last thing she needed this morning was a glimpse of Bohdi. Little was said between them after Alex turned down a ride back to the chalet once the helicopter had touched down. Alex thanked Bohdi for the day, but even she could not miss the hurt clouding those blue eyes. Alex didn't know what to do, so she did nothing and walked away. It didn't feel good, but it was the right thing to do.

Alex opened the door to Cal's office to find that the representatives from RG Holdings were already seated and waiting.

'Gentlemen.'

'Ah, Miss Mason. You're finally here. I'm Gerald Park and this is my associate, Andrew Gains. A pleasure to meet you.'

Neither man stood up, but Mr. Park did extend his hand. Alex took it and nodded at the other fellow. She had played this game before. These gentlemen viewed her as merely the daughter necessary to sign papers. In her line of work, she was used to men underestimating her. It was always a mistake on their part. Her father owned 51% of Talisman and now she did. Her decision was the only one that mattered in the end. Alex wanted the sale to go through, but she didn't need to make it easy for them. Corporate male intimidation lost its effect on her years ago.

Alex leaned against the desk in front of the two men. 'I can see you are both eager to get started.' She continued to look at their guests as she spoke to Cal. 'Cal, have you already taken Gerald and Andrew for a tour?'

'Not yet, no. We were waiting for you,' replied Cal.

They probably expected an apology, but Alex would not give them one. She wasn't late. She was never late.

'Great. Then why don't we do that first? I assume that you have both done your homework and aerial photos will be sufficient. But if you are interested, we can use the helicopter for a flyover, if you require a birds eye view of the resort.'

She flashed a bright smile at the two men. Whether they realized it or not, they were smiling back.

Gerald was the first to respond. 'That won't be necessary. A quick walk around outside and then a look at the hotel will be fine. We have indeed done our homework.'

Alex threw another beaming grin at his forced smile. She was beginning to enjoy this.

'Wonderful! Shall we?'

Alex ushered all three men out the door. Cal was looking a little nervous and jumpy, but Alex attributed that to nerves. He whispered to her as they exited, 'You're more like your father than I realized.'

She wasn't sure he was intending his words as a compliment, but Alex decided she liked the idea anyway.

While they walked the resort, Alex let Cal take the lead in answering the majority of their questions. He was well versed in all things Talisman and Alex accepted his expertise. Cal may have his issues, but he knew the resort inside and out. It gave her a chance to observe the men from RG and listen to the questions they asked and what they said to each other. There was insight to be gained by remaining silent.

The majority of their questions were a review of costs to run the lifts, the number of employees, and costs for all the non-ski related entertainment. They didn't seem overly impressed with sleighs and dogsleds, more in the outlay of expenses to provide the extras.

Their cold survey of the resort's unique elements was beginning to irritate her. Did they need a price tag on Freda as well? She understood they needed valuations, but Talisman was more than a resource that provided a solid return. They were treating it like it was another asset, like—like she was. An asset to be bought and sold.

She blamed Bohdi for this. A couple of days ago this never would have bothered her. It was a simple business deal. Now she was offended that Gus and Sophie were being discussed as part of a risk reward ratio. It wasn't the distasteful representatives that RG Holding had sent. Those guys were a dime a dozen in her world. What was happening to her?

Alex was glad when they decided to move into the hotel. Brunch was an excellent idea. Perhaps she would be less aggravated on a full stomach.

While they waited for their food to arrive, the discussion from outside continued.

'Your staff is very familiar with the guests. Is that the most efficient use of their time?' said Gerald.

Irritated, Alex spoke before Cal had a chance, 'Most of our staff speak a minimum of three languages. I think the guests appreciate the efforts of our staff. We have never had a complaint. Ever.'

'Fair enough.' Gerald looked to his partner. 'Perhaps a better question is why haven't you expanded? Your brand is doing well. Why not capitalize on that? There is a significant amount of land that is available to you.'

Alex flinched. She didn't like the direction of this conversation. They were asking legitimate questions from a company standpoint, but if they had no intention of changing Talisman, why even ask? Why the interest?

'I believe our brand is doing well *because* we haven't expanded.'

'Yes, I understand that, but you could test the waters. Clear back to the east of the resort. Develop additional hotels, hostels—'

'My father's vision was a walk-able resort.'

'My dear, it still could be. Simply shuttle them to the hill. Or build more private homes.'

Gerald's condescending tone was grating on her nerves and Alex wasn't sure why this conversation was taking place.

'I don't understand—'

Cal cleared his throat and immediately Andrew spoke. 'This isn't really important; merely curiosity on our part, right, Gerald?'

The other man agreed, 'Of course.'

Alarm bells were ringing in Alex's head. She fixed her gaze on Cal. It was too cool in the restaurant for him to be that sweaty.

'Am I missing something here, Cal? We have talked about this for over a month now. You said this was to be a simple exchange of hands, not a change in vision.'

Cal's eyes widened. 'No, of course not! You heard them yourself. It's curiosity. We have a plan, Alex, I don't see any reason not to follow through with that.' He drummed his fingers on the table and gave her a reproachful stare. 'Perhaps you have spent a bit too much time with Bohdi?'

Alex's brows snapped together, 'Bohdi?'

'Who's Bohdi?' asked Gerald.

Cal gave a dismissive wave. 'Just the owner of the T-Bar. Thinks his short-lived celebrity status allows him a say in the running of this place. Arrogant dreamer. Delusions of grandeur.'

Instantly her annoyance transformed into a seething anger. To prevent an outburst, she began tapping her fork on the table. She imagined stabbing it into Cal's hand that was resting on the table. Was Cal trying to say she was weak-minded and easily influenced? It wouldn't be the first time a man doubted her ability to think for herself. Alex couldn't decide what was bothering her more, Cal's opinion of her, or his offensive description of Bohdi.

'I am asking a reasonable question, Cal. No different than my father would do. And while Bohdi may not have ownership in Talisman itself, he does have a stake in the resort. He only wants what is best for it.'

Seriously, now Cal had her defending Bohdi. How had this gotten so turned around? Hadn't she thought the exact same thing? Why was she so offended when the words came from someone else? She watched as the three men at the table shared silent, uneasy glances. There was definitely more going on here than she realized.

'Let me be blunt, gentlemen. I want to know exactly what the intentions of RG Holdings are for Talisman.'

Gerald answered. 'Nothing drastic, extra lodging, a few tweaks here and there.'

'It's not a big deal,' Cal added.

'Why don't I believe that? What guarantee do I have?'

Alex looked around the table. Cal was fidgeting so badly she was surprised he hadn't fallen out of the chair. Gerald was about to speak when Andrew placed his hand on his arm and leaned forward.

'Miss Mason, Alex, I don't wish to be rude, but what RG Holdings does with this property is our business, not yours. I can appreciate that you have an… emotional attachment, but this is how a sale works: you get the money and we get the asset. You do not have a say in future development.' Andrew shrugged. 'Your partner has made his wishes clear and given us his commitment to this sale. Our visit here is merely a formality.'

Alex put down the fork and made a steeple of her fingers. Her eyes blazed as she spoke softly and slowly; she didn't want him to miss a word. 'Allow me to explain something to you, Andrew. My partner here only owns 49% of Talisman. Whatever assurances you think you might have obtained from him were not his to give. So… even if you buy his stake, you will never be able to make any changes without my consent. That is how this works.'

Cal's face drained of color. 'Alex—'

'Miss Mason,' Andrew interrupted. 'We were given the impression that you wished to sell the resort. That you were ready to divest of your share. What is the problem here? You have something you wish to be rid of, and we are willing to take it off your hands. Why does it matter what happens after? Are we discussing feelings or business here?'

'I don't need to explain myself to any of you. The answer is it matters. That is all you need to know. I think that I will excuse myself now, gentlemen.'

Alex rose from the shocked table. Andrew stood as well. 'I don't think you see the big picture here, Miss Mason.'

'And I don't think you realize that this conversation is over.'

Andrew shook his head. 'This is far from over. This deal will go through. I suggest you discuss the details with your partner.' He turned on Cal. 'I advise you have a heart to heart with Miss Mason here, or you will have bigger problems than a… what did she call it? Change of vision.'

Alex could feel her nostrils flare. 'Is that a threat? I certainly hope not. It would be a mistake to try and force this sale.'

'We all have our jobs to do, Miss Mason.'

There was nothing more to say. Alex needed time to discover why RG Holdings felt they had a right to her resort. Yes, her resort. Somehow in the past hour, Alex had gone from being free and clear of Talisman to becoming its champion. It wasn't what she had come here to do, but there was absolutely no chance she would let RG Holdings destroy what her father had built and what Ben had loved so dearly. It galled her to even think it, but Bohdi had been right. RG Holdings would have stripped away every piece of what made Talisman magical. She was surprised how deeply it mattered to her, but it did. She was not going to let that happen.

***

'Are you going to go out and talk to her?'

Bohdi looked back to see Jaz scrutinizing him. He was asking himself the same question. Alex looked a little hot around the collar as he watched her march out of the hotel. He took some small relief in knowing it wasn't him that had set her to stomping off this time. If her anger was a result of her meeting with the developers, even better. Maybe Alex was finally starting to understand that RG Holdings would never be interested in a boutique resort. They were a massive development company. They developed. That's what they did. It shouldn't come as surprise.

'I'm not sure she would welcome a visit right now.'

Not from him, anyway. He didn't need to say that to Jaz. She already knew something had happened between him and

Alex out on the mountain. She didn't need the details, no matter what she thought.

'Well if you do go over there, you better know what it is you want,' said Jaz.

'What does that mean?'

'Do I really need to explain it? You know exactly what I'm talking about. You've spent more time looking out these windows in the past few days than you've spent working. You have a problem and it's not Cal Stenson and RG Holdings.'

'You don't know what you're talking about.' Bohdi turned back to the window. He didn't need Jaz to see she knew exactly what she was talking about.

'No, you don't know what to do with the blonde stick of dynamite that has blown up all your plans of hiding away for the rest of your life.' Jaz headed into the kitchen. 'Take your dog for a walk. Chewie's not such a big fool.'

Bohdi didn't bother to answer Jaz. She said what she needed to say and she was already gone. Hiding. Pfft. What was Jaz even talking about? He wasn't hiding from anything. He had built a life here. He had created a place for himself; he was a part of something. Bohdi did not hold out for dreams of more, he accepted that this is how it would be. He thought he was content, until Alex Mason drove right into a snow bank and into his heart, a cruel reminder that life doesn't always meet your expectations. She didn't want him or didn't want to want him. Bohdi recognized that. He knew that even if he wished it, he would never be the one for Alex. What would he say? Let me love you? Let me be the one to take your pain, and then let me be the one to let you down. Again. Not the recipe for the happy ending that Alex deserved. She had been through enough and his desire for her did not outweigh the potential heartbreak for Alex when he failed her. And he would. Somehow, in some way, Bohdi would disappoint her. He would never be good enough for Alex.

He only wished that she could understand how much he missed Ben, that it hadn't been easy for him either, and that selling off Talisman wasn't going to ease her grief. He knew that. It was part of the reason he came back. Alex hadn't been back in 16 years and she was still angry. Didn't she see that she wasn't dealing with her grief? She was only putting off a reckoning that would one day come whether she liked it or not. Nobody has that kind of control.

Dammit. He did need to talk to her. Whatever took place in the hotel had her ticked off about something. He watched her trudge her way home through the snow. If there was a chance he could help, he should.

Bohdi called out for Chewie. He was overdue for a walk anyway. If they happened to end up in Alex's direction, then so be it. He couldn't be held responsible for the whims of a dog. He shook his head at himself. Alex may be on to something regarding his accountability.

It didn't take much encouragement for Chewie to head out the door. Bohdi refused to acknowledge the wink Jaz shot his way. The girl was too cocky for her own good and she didn't need encouragement. It didn't matter that she was consistently right.

Lost in thought, Bohdi wandered aimlessly about the resort for a while, Chewie soaking up the attentions of the children he passed. Bohdi didn't want to march directly to Alex's, but he didn't want to waste time when he could be talking with her. If she was upset as a result of her meeting with the RG Holdings reps, then he needed to capitalize on that. He wanted to let her know there were possibilities other than selling out.

Bohdi bent down to talk to Chewie. 'Listen, buddy, I need your help on this one.'

Chewie looked up to Bohdi and licked his face, one ear cocked. He was on board for whatever mission Bohdi gave him.

'I need you to go find Alex. She's at Jim's. You go find Alex, buddy. Get in the door. I'll handle the rest.' Bohdi rubbed under Chewie's collar. 'I bet she's got lots of cheese for you, delicious yummy cheese. So many treats. You go. I'll meet you there.'

With an excited bark, Chewie took off toward the chalet, Bohdi yelling after him, 'Get past the door!'

He didn't know how much Chewie actually understood, but words like "find", "treats", "Alex", and "Jim" should be enough to get Bohdi what he needed. He felt a little guilty for the underhanded maneuver. He was well aware of how effective a loveable, furry wingman could be, but it was all hands on deck right now.

Bohdi kept out of sight as he watched Chewie make his way to Alex's front door. His barking demand saw it opened immediately. Alex glanced around and then let the dog in.

'Atta boy,' muttered Bohdi. He refrained from pumping his arm in victory. His behaviour was already bordering on childish; he didn't need the guests to witness crazy as well.

He slowly walked over to the majestic chalet, shielding his eyes as though he were on the lookout for his wayward dog along the way. He didn't want his ruse to be discovered, in case she was watching. He really was becoming pathetic. He could only imagine if Jaz saw him now.

His heart was pounding when he knocked on the door. He doubted it was from the short walk over.

Alex opened the door. One eye cocked and arms crossed, she leaned against the doorway.

'Why am I not surprised?'

Bohdi gave her his best attempt at confusion. 'What? I'm looking for Chewie. Wondering if he ended up here?'

'Oh, he's here. Let me guess. Once again, this isn't your doing?' Alex wasn't going to cut him any slack.

'Listen, Chewie has a mind of his own—'

'I don't have time for this, Bohdi,' Alex stopped him from continuing. 'I've met with RG and I need to review the financials for Talisman. I've wasted too much time here already.'

'Wasted?'

'You know what I mean, Bohdi.'

'I think I'm starting to.' He shook off the offense. 'Is there anything I can do to help? We should really talk anyway. You know, about why you keep luring my dog to your side.'

Alex didn't even crack a smile. 'You're impossible. I don't want to talk. I want to get this done. And inviting you in will not help me. So, if you really want to help, please leave me alone.'

Bohdi felt the sting of her words. Alex was making it very clear where he stood in regard to her and his involvement in her decision. He wasn't enough of a masochist that he was going to beg to be let in.

'Fine, I'll take my dog.' Bohdi's smile finally slipped. 'Chew! Come here, boy!'

Chewie came to the edge of the foyer and then sat down.

'Come on. Let's go.'

Chewie sniffed the air in his direction, then lay down. Bohdi fought the urge to drag his traitorous dog out the door. What good is a wingman if he takes the girl?

He saw a brief flash of apology cross Alex's face.

'I don't mind if he stays,' she said.

Bohdi looked from his dog to Alex, accepting he wasn't going to convince either one of them right now.

'Fine. Send him home when you've had enough. He knows the way.'

Bohdi turned and stomped down the stairs. He could feel Alex's eyes on his back, but he didn't turn around. He heard the door close and he knew that it was him she was shutting out.

CHAPTER THIRTEEN

Alex pressed her back against the door, fighting the urge to open it and yell at Bohdi to come back. Instead she looked at Chewie, wondering if Bohdi's dog had an agenda all of his own.

She walked over to scratch his head. 'What are you up to, dog? Be up front. Tell me you only want treats. I don't think I can handle anymore underhanded behavior today.'

Chewie's tail started to thump against the floor at treats, so Alex walked to the kitchen with Chewie close behind.

After a handful of cut cheese, Alex put an end to Chewie's snack. The last thing she needed was to make the poor pup sick. Bohdi was already irritated with her. A dog with a stomach-ache would only add insult to the injury she had thrown at the man today.

Curled up with her laptop, Alex began to sort through the different files on Talisman. Everything was in order. The statements were clean, and Cal's work was precise and consistent over the years. The resort was more than profitable, and even with increased expenditures for improvements made over the years, they were always back in the black quickly. There was no debt for RG Holdings to assume. She could understand why they wanted it. Her financial analysis revealed only positive findings for cash flow, sales volume, debt capacity, and potential for growth.

The last was the most likely reason they were hungry for the resort. It was also the reason her father never sold. The return on their investment was more than significant. They didn't need to change anything in order to make money. At what point does it become a matter of greed? RG was exactly like the companies she was so tired of dealing with in her line of work. More was never enough. That didn't matter now; she wasn't going to sell her share to them and even if Cal did, they couldn't make any changes without her buy-in. So really, everything looked to be in order. There was nothing that raised any red flags for her. Only one thing had caught her eye. It wasn't a big deal, nothing that indicated an issue, more of a surprise than anything.

Over the past year Cal had increased the dividends that Talisman was paying him. It wasn't a problem, but it was unusual. Both her father and Cal had taken a business salary along with dividends over the years. The last year Cal had increased his significantly. It wasn't an indicator of foul play or business difficulties, but in Alex's experience, anyone increasing their take that much had some serious personal problems.

It was no wonder that Cal was so eager to make this sale to RG Holdings. Something was going on with the man. He was obviously in need of cash. Why had he been acting so jumpy since she arrived? Alex initially attributed it to being overworked and overwhelmed, but she never should have ignored it. Alex needed to talk to him. A real talk, the one that they should have had from the beginning. If she was going to be able to help him, she needed him to be honest about what was going on. Since Alex had no intention of selling to RG, not after their discussion at the hotel, she would need to figure out a solution that would work for Cal.

'What do you think, Chewie? What am I supposed to do? How did it all get so screwed up?

The retriever jumped up to join Alex on the couch, tunnelling his nose under her arm to lift it up, his sole focus to have her pet him.

'Guess it all seems pretty simple to you. Do what feels right. Problem is, I can't even tell what that is anymore. I don't know what to think. It's not as cut and dried as I thought.'

Alex absently rubbed Chewie as she tried to figure out what to do. As long as she kept petting him, he was content to let her think as long as she needed to.

She looked down to her furry companion, who in response flipped over so she could have full access to rub his belly.

'You're shameless,' she scolded and scratched him anyway. 'I need to talk to Cal, and you need to go home. Before Bohdi decides to come back here and demand your release.'

Alex had to shove the retriever off her leg. Chewie wasn't ready to give up the attention, but Alex had work to do.

By the time she threw her jacket and boots on, Chewie conceded defeat and joined her on the hike back to the resort.

As they walked, Alex took a real look around the resort. She took in her surroundings with open eyes for the first time since she had been back. When she initially arrived, she had appreciated what her father had created, but with RG Holdings' threat of change, she was finally understanding its worth. The intimacy of the resort was what gave Talisman that magical feel. Shuttles of tourists, endless hotels, and condos would destroy it all.

She needed to find a buyer that understood that and would maintain the vision that had been so purposefully shaped. She could delay selling, but that didn't help Cal. Her father's business partner was clearly in trouble and Alex wanted to help him. He had been at her father's side for years, loyal despite their differences, and he deserved her support.

Despite being lost in her thoughts Alex was instantly aware of Bohdi's presence; the tingle that ran over every inch of her skin was the giveaway. He was standing outside the T-Bar, watching her. He was too far away so she would need to shout if she wanted to speak to him. But she didn't. She didn't know what to say. Everything Alex thought she knew about Bohdi was wrapped in an ugly, tangled, confused mess. Suddenly life wasn't so black and white. That's why she needed to get out of this place. Sort out Cal, worry about the sale later, and get far away from the soul-piercing blue eyes of Bohdi Vonn.

It was Chewie that came to her rescue. When he saw Bohdi, he ran toward him. Stopping halfway, Chewie looked back at Alex and barked, encouraging her to follow. When she didn't, the retriever continued on to Bohdi, who welcomed him with a pat on the rump and ushered him inside. Neither Bohdi nor Chewie bothered to look back.

Alex wanted to pretend it didn't hurt. But she had only herself to lie to, and that was becoming exhausting. She couldn't deal with the myriad of emotions that Bohdi stirred within her, especially the ones that caused her to catch her breath at the very sight of him. She needed to deal with Cal. That was the only thing she should be worrying about.

***

Bohdi stomped up the stairs that led to his loft above the T-Bar. His face must have reflected the turmoil and frustration he felt because Jaz stared, but she didn't say a word.

He paced the floors until he had worn a path and then plunked his body onto his couch. He cradled his head in his hands until Chewie jumped up beside him, the dog's forceful attempts to crawl over him and snuggle in providing comfort.

'What am I supposed to do, buddy? I want to wrap her in my arms and never let her go. Kiss her until neither one of us remembers why it is such a bad idea.'

Chewie grumbled.

'I know! I also want to throw her on the next plane out of here. The last thing we need is a constant reminder of what will never be.'

Bohdi looked down at his dog and received a lick across his cheek for his efforts. 'Sure, you want her to stay, because she likes you.' Chewie whined. 'No, it's true. Even if there is a small, tiny part of her that still likes me, there is a much larger part that wants to be rid of me. And I can't say I blame her.'

He knew it was crazy. How could he reconcile falling for Ben's little sister? Was it the sparks that flew from the first moment they met on the road? Or their shared history that connected them in a way he had never felt before? Why was he even entertaining the possibility? He had let the Mason family down in the worst of ways once before. Did he really want to risk hurting Alex all over again? Was his desire for love and redemption more important than Alex's need to move on?

No, he had done enough damage. Jim may have told him time and again that he wasn't to blame, that the accident was not his fault. Jim was a good man, a forgiving man. And though Jim may have given him absolution in Ben's death, Bohdi could never forgive himself. It was in the quiet moments that Bohdi had been witness to Jim's pain, when Jim thought no one was watching. The way his fingers would unconsciously touch a picture frame as Jim walked down the hall. Heartbreak that never fades for a father who has lost his son. Bodhi carried that weight with the knowledge that if he'd done more it could have changed everything.

Everything. But he hadn't and there was nothing he could do about it.

Head in Bohdi's lap, Chewie's ears suddenly perked up, and the retriever hopped from the couch and sprang to the window. It was the whining that forced Bohdi from his misery on the couch. He pushed aside the curtain to see Alex walking towards the chalet. It looked like she was wiping away tears. His heart clenched at the thought. The idea of Alex in any more pain was more than he could bear. He longed to go after her, but he knew better now. She didn't want him there. She wanted her space to deal with, or more likely, to avoid her problems. Alex made it very clear she did not want his help.

Chewie whined again and nudged at Bohdi. 'Nah, not this time, Chew.'

Bohdi left the window and went over to the laptop on his coffee table. He wanted a distraction and work still needed to get done. He stared at the same purchase order for five minutes before he pushed away from the table.

Who was he kidding? Alex may not want to see him, but Cal might be able to provide some insight. He and Cal were often at odds, but that didn't mean Bohdi couldn't get some answers out of him.

An exhausting hour later, Bohdi left Cal's office only to see Freda running towards him. The little woman looked concerned.

'What's wrong?' Bohdi asked.

'It's Alex. She's heading up the lift. She looked so upset. I asked her what was wrong, but she said she needed to clear her head. That there was something she needed to do.'

'Dammit!'

'I'm worried—'

'It's okay. I'll head up now. I have a feeling I know where she is going.'

'Do you want me to send Arlo too?'

Bohdi did his best to reassure her. ‘It’s okay. I’ll find her, Freda. I’ll bring her back. I promise.’

‘Then go.’ Freda gave Bohdi a push. ‘Alex needs you, even if she doesn’t realize it.’

Bohdi didn’t bother to dispute Freda’s observation. He ran back to the T-Bar to grab his gear. If Alex was headed where he thought she was, he needed to hurry. The weather had been warm throughout the day and with the heavy snowfall from last night there were places on the mountain that weren’t safe. Alex was an excellent skier, but she had no avalanche training and he wasn’t willing to risk her safety just because she didn’t want to talk to him. From Freda’s description, Bohdi wasn’t sure if Alex was even thinking straight. After his talk with Cal, he didn’t blame her.

Bohdi needed to reach her. If something were to happen to Alex—No, nothing was going to happen. He wouldn’t let it.

CHAPTER FOURTEEN

Alex was so angry she could barely see. She watched her hands shake as they pushed up the safety bar of the lift. The truth was it wasn't only anger. It was betrayal, guilt, and confusion. It was a chaotic explosion of emotion and she was ill prepared to deal with it. Alex had spent so long compartmentalizing her feelings that when all the doors opened at once she was a complete disaster. She was at a loss what to do or even believe anymore.

Nothing made sense. She hadn't been content, but she had grown comfortable with the beliefs and perceptions she had of Talisman, her father, and Bohdi. There was so much that she hadn't realized. So much that had been coloured by her mother's pain. So much that she hadn't even tried to understand.

Cal's betrayal was the final straw. People weren't simple; she knew that but never truly understood it. Sitting in her father's home, the place that had once been a source of warmth and love, Alex knew that she needed to face the true source of the pain that had changed the course of all of their lives, and it wasn't only Bohdi. She needed to step back in time. She had never been back to the run where Ben died. Alex couldn't remember if she had ever wanted to, but it didn't matter; she wasn't given a choice. Her mother made sure of it.

But it was time now to rip off the Band-Aid she had placed over the injury to her heart and examine the wound beneath. There was only one place to do so. She needed to see where Ben died.

Alex skied across the hill through a short, treed, and narrow pathway that led to the double diamond run. She had been here only a few times before and only once had she attempted the run. It was in an effort to prove that she wasn't a child to Ben and Bohdi. She had been an impetuous child and lucky to have made it down in one piece. It wasn't merely the steep nature of the pitch. It was the rugged terrain that gave it the advanced rating. When her brother had discovered her foolishness, he had yelled at her for her stupidity. It was one of the reasons she knew that it must have been Bohdi's idea to take the run that day. If Ben thought it so dangerous for her in good weather, then she knew he never would have made the decision to ride it that day. Not after such a huge storm the night before. Would he?

It was the sign, not the landscape, that first caught her attention. When they originally named the run, it was Bandito's Way. Ben had changed it at some point to "Bendito's Way" with a black Sharpie. It looked like someone had made that change permanent. The sign was professionally renamed after her brother.

'Oh, Ben.' Alex didn't bother to wipe at the tears that were starting to form in the corners of her eyes.

She skied up to the tape stretched across the entrance to the run to take a look at the rugged terrain that had taken her brother's life. After the heavy snowfall from the night before, public access was not allowed. That didn't matter; she didn't come to ski the course. Alex came to face her fears. It was here from where so many of her fears stemmed.

There were no other skiers around and for that Alex was grateful. It was the silence she sought. Time to think, no interruptions. She needed to figure out what her plan was going to be. Cal's news threw her for a loop, and if she was going to help him and send RG Holdings packing, she had better think fast. Even if she was successful in preventing the sale to the developer, then what? Was she holding on to her stake and staying here at Talisman? How exactly did she plan on solving the problem of Bohdi Vonn?

She was torn between hating him for his part in Ben's death and loving him despite it. Even if what happened hadn't been his fault, the accident changed the direction of her life. How do you simply forget that? As long as she stayed here, she would be connected to Bohdi and she could never move on. Alex needed to steel her heart against him. She had done it once. She could do it again.

Leaning on her poles and staring out at the snow, Alex heard the rumble of a snowmobile engine. When she saw the flash of Bohdi's jacket as the rider rounded into the pathway, she wanted to scream. What was he doing here? Why couldn't he leave her alone?

'Alex!' Bohdi tossed his helmet to the side. 'What are you doing out here?'

'Stop! Just stop. I don't want to talk to you. I want to be left alone.' She edged closer to the tape, as her words weren't slowing Bodhi down. 'Please leave me alone.'

Bohdi held up one hand. 'Okay. Fine. Then come back down with me.' He pointed to the tape. 'It's not safe. Come back down. I'll drop you off at the chalet. No one will bother you.'

'Don't talk to me like I'm a child. I'm not 13 anymore.'

'Then stop acting like one. Get over here.'

'I don't need you telling me what to do. I can take care of myself.' Alex could feel her anger mounting, like a bomb set to explode.

'I know you can. You've been pretty damn clear about that,' barked Bohdi. 'That has nothing to do with this. Get over here.'

'No.'

'Get over here, Alex.'

'I said no. Did you not hear me?'

'Oh, I heard you. I'm just ignoring you because you are being ridiculous.'

'You don't have the right to order me around.' Who did he think he was?

Bohdi looked heavenward. 'Are you kidding me? You're as stubborn as Ben was.'

'Go to hell, Bohdi,' snarled Alex. 'You don't have a clue what this is about. You have no idea.' Alex ferociously wiped away a traitorous tear.

He watched her for a moment before he responded with a sigh. 'I do know,' his voice softened. 'I talked to Cal, Alex. He told me everything.'

'Did he tell you he's been taking money from RG. That they've been feeding him cash to seal this deal? Did he tell you that?'

'Yes, he knows he screwed up. He feels awful about what he's done.'

'Feels awful? He feels awful? He should feel awful; now I have to find a way to keep Cal out of jail and still find a way to thwart the deal with RG,' responded Alex. 'They're going to destroy this place, you know. You were right. Does that make you happy now? They plan to turn this into another resort for the masses. Everything that makes Talisman special will be gone.'

Bohdi took another step towards her. 'Come on. We will figure it out. But you need to come with me.'

Alex scoffed, 'Come with you? I don't think so.' She pointed her gloved finger at him. 'You're the reason for all of this.'

His eyes widened at her accusation. 'Me? You're blaming all of this on me? I tried to warn you about RG. I told you they were a money-hungry corporation. I can't believe you're surprised.'

'I'm not talking about them. They're the last straw. I'm talking about it all.'

'It all? What does that mean?'

'You.' Alex ducked under the tape, moving further away from Bohdi, onto the run. 'If you hadn't convinced Ben to ski out here… if Ben hadn't died… none of this would be happening. I would have been around to see what was happening to Cal. I would have known Dad was unwell. I might have fixed this. But I didn't even have a chance.'

Bohdi looked at her in stunned silence.

Alex couldn't believe she had finally said the words. For a moment she debated taking them back, but what was the point? It was an ugly truth that was hanging between them and there was no point in pretending otherwise. She blamed him for her brother's death and that was too big an obstacle to ignore.

He shook his head. 'No. No way, Alex. I'm guilty of a lot of things. You're right about that, but not about Jim. You could have shown up here anytime. Your father would have welcomed you with open arms. You made the choice to stay away. That's not on me.'

'Maybe, but that doesn't change what happened with Ben,' said Alex. 'It crushed me, Bohdi. My family was torn apart. I didn't know how to deal with that. I didn't know what to do. So, while you went on to become the country's darling, gaining accolades wherever you went, I learned to close myself off from people. I never want to feel heartbreak like that again.'

Bohdi's mouth opened then closed again. He looked defeated. A twinge of regret passed through her.

'You're right. It doesn't change anything. I know that. But what's your plan? Sell everything and live on a beach somewhere? You prefer to be surrounded by strangers?

Those people will never understand your pain the way that we do here. That I do.'

'That you do? What do you know? You didn't lose a brother that day. You didn't watch the agony of your mother as she railed against the world over the loss of her son. You carried on, doing what you loved. Like nothing had happened. Understand my pain? You have no idea what I have been through, Mr. Olympics. Your life never skipped a beat.'

Eyes flashing, Bohdi took another step towards her. She could see the muscles jumping in his jaw.

'You know what, Alex? Maybe I don't understand all of those things, but here's what you don't seem to get. You lost a brother that day, but I also lost my best friend.'

'Then maybe you never should have brought him up here. You had to know it wasn't safe.'

'Me?' Bohdi looked incredulous. 'What are you saying? Don't you think I tried to stop him? Do you even remember what your brother was like?'

'How dare you. I knew my brother—'

'You should. You're just like him. Look at you now. What the hell are you even doing up here?'

'You have no right. No right to say those things about Ben. I remember him perfectly.'

'You remember him with a child's memory, Alex. Have you forgotten the daredevil that broke at least one bone every summer, only to heal in time for ski season? I'm not going to stand here and pretend I wasn't along for the ride, but most of the time it was because I couldn't stop the train. It was always fun, until one day it wasn't. If I could go back, I would. I wish I had tried harder to stop him.'

'Why didn't you?' cried Alex.

'I don't know. I'm sorry.'

Alex didn't know what to think. Was Bohdi right? Her memory was skewed on so many other things… was this one of them? Her mother had been so angry and Bohdi was an easy target. He was alive, and her son was not. Her father never held Bohdi responsible. Did her mother's intense grief require a scapegoat? Was that Bohdi?

She should be asking him. Hear the truth straight from Bohdi's mouth. She had heard only small snippets of the surrounding circumstances of Ben's death in her mother's rants. Nothing he told her should be a surprise. So why was she so afraid to ask him? Was it deep down she knew that Bohdi wasn't really to blame, or was it her heart that didn't want it to be true? The idea she could be wrong made her feel incredibly uncomfortable. Either way, she was dreading the answer.

'What do you need, Alex? Do you want to know what happened?'

'I already know what happened. My mother explained everything. You convinced him to take this run, and then you kept skiing while Ben… while he…' She couldn't finish.

'I failed Ben, but not like that. Ben wanted to ski Bandito, not me. I should have tried harder to stop him. The heavy snowstorm the night before made it way too dangerous around those trees, never mind avalanche conditions. He wanted me to go first. He liked to make sure he outdid me, and he always did. When I came to a stop, Ben wasn't behind me. I thought he was still at the top. That he hadn't started yet. So I waited.'

Bohdi's eyes had glazed over, lost in the memory of his words.

'He didn't show, and I started to panic. I looked across the slope. That's when I saw them. The backs of Ben's skis under one of the massive spruce trees. That's when I knew he was caught in a tree well.'

Alex remained silent, horrified by the detail Bohdi was sharing.

'I knocked off my skis, but the snow was so deep, the hill too steep. I climbed the hill, desperate to reach him. Every two steps forward had me sliding one back. I couldn't get there fast enough. Once I got to him, I started digging, but the snow kept falling in. There was so much snow.' Bohdi didn't hide the stream of tears that ran down his cheeks. 'When I finally reached his face, I knew I was too late.'

'Bohdi—'

'I tried, Alex. I tried to breathe life back into him. But he was gone. We didn't have a radio. What was I going to do? Leave him up here? I couldn't.'

'Oh no. Oh, Bohdi.' Hot tears streamed down Alex's face.

'I carried him. I skied down with my best friend in my arms. I can't remember how long it took. It felt like a lifetime.' Bohdi wiped the tears from his face. 'So, you don't need to remind me of my role. I know how badly I screwed up. If I could have convinced him not to ski the run, if I hadn't waited, if I climbed faster, dug faster. I live with that every day. I still carry him with me… every day.'

'Bohdi—'

'No. No my life isn't perfect, Alex. You ever wonder why I never won a bloody gold medal? Why it was always out of reach?'

Alex held up her hands. 'It's okay, Bohdi.'

He didn't stop. 'We were supposed to go the Olympics together. Ben and Bohdi on the podium, together. He was always the better skier. I knew that, we both did. That's why, Alex. I could live our dream for the both of us, but I could never take the gold. That prize would always be Ben's.'

The air between them was still. Alex didn't know what to say. His shocking revelation of the events leading to Ben's death were almost too much to bear. But it also made sense. It explained her father's lack of resentment towards Bohdi.

Perhaps the pain her mother felt was easier to handle if she had someone to blame.

She wanted to say something to ease the pain that Bohdi felt. Tell him that he wasn't to blame. That Ben's death wasn't his fault. How she was wrong, she had been all along. But how does one justify years of undeserved condemnation?

It didn't matter when she loved him back then and didn't matter that she loved him now. And she did love him. Her heart had never truly let Bohdi go. But there was too much pain between them. She had been so wrong, and she had let too much time pass.

'All this time… I didn't know, Bohdi. My mother—it doesn't matter. I didn't know. I didn't try to understand.' Alex knew there was no point in trying to explain the past several years. How her mother's grief had impacted her. It was irrelevant and the damage was already done.

'I'm sorry for what I said. It wasn't fair. You're right, there is a lot that I have forgotten or chose to forget. You were so young. I can't even begin to imagine what you went through that day.'

'I'm not telling you to make you feel sorry for me. I don't deserve any pity. I only want you to understand.'

She understood. She understood that Bohdi held himself responsible for the accident, the same way she had, the same way her mother blamed him. How could he forgive her for compounding his hurt with her accusations?

'I was wrong. It wasn't your fault. You didn't have a chance. My father knew that, Bohdi. I hope you do too.'

'Whatever. All I know is I'm trying. I'm trying to move forward. Live like Ben would have wanted. Create a life in one of the most beautiful places in the world. I know I'm not perfect, but at least I'm making an effort. Maybe if we—'

'No, Bohdi, don't. If I had known, maybe things could be different. But I can't keep loving you. This needs to end.

Even knowing what I do now doesn't change anything. It's too late.' She inwardly screamed at herself for being a liar as she watched his face fall. She wished she could give him more. Why was she still so afraid to open her heart to him, to love, to life?

'Of course not. I was a fool to even think it. You go then. Stay one step ahead of the pain. How's that working for you so far?'

His words stung. But the truth hurts and, even though he wasn't wrong, it still bothered her.

'That's not fair! I'm trying too, Bohdi.'

'You're not trying. You're running. There's a difference.'

'I do what I need to do,' said Alex.

'You can't shut everyone out. Eventually it will catch up with you. You can't outrun pain.'

Alex shuffled closer to Bohdi, the safety tape still between them. 'Let me guess, staying here with you classifies as not running? You're the only one that can ease my pain.'

She wanted him to say yes. To yell at her for being so stubborn. To convince her it was worth the risk to her heart.

Bohdi shook his head. 'No. You were right about us. And what you do is none of my business. If you want to go, go. I won't be the one standing in the way of your dreams. But if you aren't selling to RG Holdings, then consider selling your share to me.'

***

'To you? Why would I do that? What are you even talking about? How can you afford that?' The shock on her face would have been comical at any other time.

'Are you really that surprised by my success?' He held up a hand. 'Don't answer that. The point is you're free to go.'

Alex didn't look as happy as he thought she would be at his words. She looked irritated; no, that wasn't it. She looked disappointed.

'I know I'm free to go. You don't have to tell me that. But what about Cal? He could end up in prison if RG decides to pursue this. They may not get the resort, but they will destroy Cal. I can't let that happen.'

'How is that your problem? You wanted to close this chapter of your life. A clean break. Isn't that what you said? Sorting out Cal's personal issues isn't your concern.'

'That's not how I wanted this—'

'You have an easy option, Alex.' He was tired of arguing with her. 'So please, come back over here. Let's go back down the mountain. I don't want to fight with you anymore. Honestly, I just want this all to be done. I will help Cal. We don't need you.'

Alex drew back like she had been slapped. He didn't want to hurt her. Bohdi immediately regretted his choice of words but he was exhausted. Reliving those last moments with Ben had taken all his strength. He couldn't do this anymore.

If Alex had given him even the slightest glimmer of hope, he would have confessed that he was a liar. That he did need her. That he needed her to stay, that he needed her to love him, and that he needed her at this side if he ever hoped to find peace again. But she hadn't. So he needed to let her go. In the end it would be for the best.

She stared at him a moment longer before she tilted her chin once more in defiance.

'Fine,' she said, then ducked back under the tape.

'Fine.'

Bohdi exhaled with relief as she walked over to his snowmobile. He took a full breath for the first time since she had edged onto the slope. The conditions were ripe for an avalanche and the fresh snow would have created deeper tree wells. There was no way he could have let her take that run. Throwing her over his shoulder would have been his last resort, but it was a step he was prepared to take. Thankfully, she came willingly.

He locked her skis into the rack on the side of his sled. She slid in behind and wrapped her arms around his waist. When she gave him a squeeze to let him know she was ready, it took all his strength not to turn around and pull her into his arms and never let her go.

The ride down was too short. Bohdi wanted her body pressed against him, if only for a moment longer. But he was out of time.

He dropped her off at the chalet and said, 'I'm assuming we don't have to do this in person. Send me the appropriate papers. That way we don't need to see each other again and you can leave sooner. Don't worry about Cal. I'll figure something out.'

Alex looked at him and pursed her lips. 'I haven't agreed to sell to you.'

Staring back, Bohdi sighed, 'You will. It gets you everything you want.'

He didn't wait for her response. He took off, heading for home. Why look back? Visions of Alex Mason would already be haunting him for the rest of his life.

CHAPTER FIFTEEN

Bohdi forced a smile on his face as he walked through the T-Bar, nodding at the afternoon's patrons. Luckily no one stopped him, so he quickly made his way up the stairs. Chewie greeted him at the top.

He barely had time to start feeling sorry for himself, when he heard the door to his loft open. Bohdi could hear it was Jaz before she came into view.

'So?' Jaz sat down on his couch, making herself comfortable. 'What gives?'

'I can't do this right now, Jaz.'

'When would you? After she sells the place? After she leaves? Or maybe you prefer to hide out here forever. You tell me.'

'I'm not hiding, Jaz! I tried. I went up there and I spilled my guts out to her and she said… whatever, I can't remember exactly what she said, but it was definitely a no.'

'So, she made the deal with RG?' asked Jaz.

'No, no, thankfully she came to her senses about that. When they met this morning, she was able to see through them. We have that at least.' Bohdi gave his friend a half-hearted smile.

'So, what's the no?'

'Me, I'm the no. I told her everything. What happened that day with Ben, all of it,' said Bohdi.

'And she still blames you? That's not right.'

'I could understand if she did, but no, she doesn't. She said it wasn't my fault. That Jim knew it, and she knows that too. At least she does now. She said I shouldn't blame myself. I don't know why, but she apologized. I told her she didn't need to. She wasn't wrong to feel that way.'

Bohdi pulled up a chair and placed his feet on the coffee table between them. 'She's leaving, Jaz.'

'So, when you told her that you love her, she said it means nothing and she's leaving? Gotta say, that's pretty cold.'

'Alex isn't cold and I don't lov—'

The scowl on Jaz's face stopped him cold. There was no point in denying it.

'Okay, fine, yeah, I love her. And no, I didn't say that… what's the point? She doesn't want to be here. She said it doesn't change anything. It's too late to keep loving me or something like that.'

Jaz exhaled deeply in his direction. She was younger and half his size, but she had a way of making him feel like an errant child.

'Alright. Then she's staying here, not selling?'

'No! Aren't you listening?'

'I'm trying but you're not making any sense.' Jaz folded her arms as her eyes bored into him.

'She doesn't want to be around me. How I feel doesn't matter.' Bohdi was getting frustrated. 'I told her I would buy her share of Talisman, that we didn't need her, that she was free to go.'

Jaz let out a long, low whistle. 'You're gonna buy… let me see if I have this right. You didn't tell her how you really feel, that you loved her, instead told her that you, in fact, no one here needed her, and that she should be on her way. That sound right?'

'Well, when you say it like that…'

'Like what? Like you're a bloody idiot? Because if that is what it sounds like, it's because that's exactly what I'm saying. She didn't reject you, Bohdi. You chased her off.'

Bohdi stared silently at Jaz as he took in her words and played over the scene with Alex in his mind. Was Jaz right? Again? Even if she was, did it matter? What if he wasn't enough? He never had been.

He had given his all and he couldn't save Ben. With all the effort he had put into his Olympic training he could never get gold. He never measured up. What made him think he was enough for Alex?

His voice was rough as he spoke, 'It doesn't matter, Jaz. It's over.'

Jaz scoffed at him. 'Look at you packing a sad over there. You keep hiding like this, you're going to be miserable and alone forever.'

'I'm not hiding, Jaz.'

She stood up and looked over at him with pity. 'Yeah, maybe you don't hide your pretty face from the world, Bohdi Vonn, but you sure hide your heart. You're afraid of getting what you want. You think you don't deserve it. You hide from anything real. A wink and smile is your game. Make people feel good, but don't let them in. You're afraid.'

'Enough, Jaz,' warned Bohdi.

'Yeah, Bohdi, you are enough. How many people have to tell you that before you start to believe it? You could have gone back to train again after you hurt your knee. Hell, you could have easily won gold. But you were afraid to take what you wanted, because you didn't think you deserved it. Same goes for the girl.'

Jaz started towards the stairs. 'She doesn't blame you. Jim never blamed you. Straight up, it's been long enough. Maybe it's time you forgave yourself.'

Bohdi didn't respond. He closed his eyes as he listened to Jaz's familiar gait as she walked down the stairs.

Once again Jaz was right. It would be difficult. His guilt was like a toxic friend. Sometimes it takes a little longer to realize it is only keeping you down. He had been using it like a crutch and he needed to stop. If Alex could forgive him, then he needed to forgive himself. It was time.

The pull between them out on the mountain wasn't simply the magic of their environment. They were connected to each other. They shared heartbreak, but they also shared a passion that ran deeper than the pain. And the pain was something they could move past, together. Alex loved him even when she thought the worst of him. Isn't that what she said? She couldn't "keep" loving him. It was that realization that gave him hope. She was worried it was too late and that too much time had passed. She was wrong. Alex didn't need to be afraid. The only thing they needed to fear was spending another moment apart.

Bohdi stood up. He could only imagine the laugh Ben would have to see how the tables turned. To see his best friend with his little sister. Maybe that is how it was always meant to be. Ben would have loved it. Bohdi knew that now.

He threw his jacket back on. He needed to convince Alex to gamble on him. That the risk would be worth it. That it was safe to open her heart to him. That he would never let her down. That they could heal together. He wasn't letting her leave until she heard him out. This was his chance, the opportunity to win something worth so much more than a gold medal. This time he would not fail. He was going to win the girl.

***

Bohdi was right. She would sell Talisman to him. He was right about a lot of things, and she had been wrong, dreadfully wrong.

But that didn't matter right now. Alex compartmentalized her feelings and pushed aside thoughts of Bohdi. She needed to solve the problem of Cal and RG Holdings. That was her focus. There was no way that Alex could, in good conscience, let Cal suffer at their hands. He had made mistakes, but he wasn't a horrible person. He simply married the wrong women. Both his ex-wives had taken him for all he was worth. He could barely keep up on alimony payments. His mistake was marrying for beauty over substance. Looking for a quick payday, he played the stock market and lost, falling deeper in debt. He was a fool, but he didn't deserve to be behind bars.

It didn't take her too long to decide how to handle RG Holdings. Alex had worked with and opposed companies like them before. If they were willing to pay off one person, they were willing to pay off others. This meant that somewhere, deep in their financials, there would be a record of it. She had enough connections with her work that with one phone call, a government audit could be started. A small army of accountants combing through their books would be a nightmare for them. She didn't need to actually do it. She only needed to imply she would if they didn't back off. Talisman would not be worth that kind of exposure to them. They would walk away. Cal would be safe.

The issue of RG Holdings and Cal was solved, but Alex still didn't feel better. She was getting everything she wanted. So why wasn't she happier?

Alex was about to tuck into the corner of the familiar couch for comfort when there was a knock at the door. She jumped up and ran to answer it.

'Oh,' sighed Alex as she let Freda in.

'Oh? That's not much of a welcome. Were you hoping for someone else?'

Alex wasn't willing to admit to Freda or herself who she had been hoping for.

'I'm sorry, come in.'

Freda didn't take off her boots, but she closed the large door behind her. 'I can't stay long. I wanted to make sure you were alright. I was worried, so I sent Bohdi after you.'

So that's how Bohdi knew.

'He found me.'

Freda looked up at her. 'I can see that. But what happened? Something is wrong.'

'It's nothing, Freda,' replied Alex. 'But I'm leaving. Bohdi has offered to buy me out and I'm going to take him up on his offer. Things with RG didn't go well. I'm not selling to them.'

'You know, Ally, you're Benny through and through. You may have your mother's beauty, but you have the same look when you're hiding something, just like your brother did. I will never forget it. I saw that look often enough.' Freda chuckled at the memory. 'He could charm his way out of almost anything. But he could never hide from me. I still miss that boy.'

'You do?'

'Of course! Don't you?' Freda seemed surprised by the question.

Alex tried to explain, 'I do. Of course, I do. Maybe it's more that I don't like to think about it.'

Freda grabbed her hand and squeezed it. 'You should. Not doing so doesn't make it hurt any less. Trust me on that. I know it's overwhelming. At such a young age you've experienced more loss and heartache than most. Unfortunately, when we live with anger and fear too long, we can become afraid to live without it. To open our hearts can be frightening.'

Alex pinched the bridge of her nose and squeezed her eyes shut before she responded. 'It's too late, Freda. I've made a huge mistake. More than one. And I can't turn back time.'

'Ally. Know this. Your father loved you. It's why he wanted you to have Talisman. He knew you didn't need the money. You needed to find your way.'

'I know I do.' Alex could feel the tears pricking at her eyelids. 'That is why I need to move on. Selling Talisman will give me the freedom to walk away from my life in the city. I'm tired of the people, my work there. I need the change.'

Freda shook her head. 'No. You're not tired of your work. That's not what is pulling you down. You're tired of fighting your heart. Your grief and sadness will be there, no matter how fast and far you try to run from it. Not because it is chasing you, but because it's shaping you. Like it has shaped Bohdi.'

'Maybe you're right, Freda. I don't know, but why didn't Dad talk to me, say this to me?'

'Would you have listened? He gave this to you because he hoped that you would come back. It was his gentle nudge. He wanted you to remember what it is to love something again. He knew you loved it here once. He wanted you to feel that again. Truthfully, I think that he secretly wished you would connect with Bohdi. That maybe you would find a way to once again love the mountain and the man Bohdi became.'

Alex didn't know how to respond to that. It was clear that her father had cared deeply for Bohdi and the feeling was mutual. But did her father really think that there was any chance that she and Bohdi would find their way to each other? If that was true, then she was letting him down one last time.

'It's impossible, Freda. I have made such a mess of things. There is no reset button on life. I've let too much time go by and I don't see how we can forget all that has happened.'

'You don't need to forget. You only need to forgive. That's how you move on.' Freda opened the front door. 'But that's enough out of me. You need some time.'

'Thank you, Freda.'

'I don't need a thank you. But please make sure you stop by before you leave.' The little woman moved to the tips of her toes to give Alex a kiss on the cheek. 'Think about what I said.'

Alex nodded, and Freda slipped out the door.

If Freda was right and her father wanted to make her feel something again, he had been more than successful. She was running a gauntlet of emotions.

Being with Bohdi yesterday, out on the mountain, brought back memories that were long forgotten. She had been reminded of what it felt like to be free. It was a part of her that had been missing over the years. There was something about being around people who were real, who knew her story, who genuinely cared for her.

Here she wasn't a showpiece for her mother's high society functions, surrounded by people who always wanted more, exactly like her clients. It, whatever it was, was never enough, for any of them.

But here it was different. Bohdi had shown her how to connect to a part of her that had been buried. The part that could lead her on the path to healing. Bohdi knew that. He warned her that running away could never provide the healing she needed. She needed Talisman, her home, and she needed Bohdi.

Bohdi had rekindled not only a passion in her body but renewed her passion for life. He reminded her of who she really was. That there was still more to this life if she was willing to open herself to it. And she was. It scared her, but she was ready to risk it, with Bohdi. If he was willing to try, then she knew she could too.

She knew she needed to talk to him. Alex wanted Bohdi to know that she did want to stay. To let him know that she didn't mean what she said. That it wasn't too late. Not yet.

She grabbed her jacket, opened the front door, and froze.

It was Bohdi.

'Alex.' His voice was rough, his breathing ragged, like he had run all the way to her door.

'Bohdi.' She could hear the waver in her voice. Alex was about to put it all on the line. But if it meant she would be with Bohdi, it was worth the risk.

He pushed past her into the chalet and closed the door behind him. He grabbed her jacket and threw it on the bench.

'Don't kick me out. I have something to say, and you need to hear it.'

'So do I—'

'Just let me say this. For once, don't try and control anything.'

By habit, Alex wanted to protest. But Bohdi looked so earnest, she obliged and remained silent.

'I don't want you to go. No, that's not even it. I need you to stay. Please don't leave me, Alex.'

As he spoke, Alex could feel the closed petals of her heart starting to bloom. Warmth spread through her as he continued to speak.

'If you go, I won't make it. I have been wandering around for years now. Searching for something that could fill the hollow in my heart. I thought being back here would fill that space. It helped, but I still wasn't whole. There was always something missing. But I learned to accept it. I thought I could learn to live without whatever that was. But the moment you walked back into my life I knew I was in trouble. I couldn't go back to pretending. What I was missing was you.'

He paused, searching her face, then continued.

'I know you're scared, so am I. But this… this is real. We know what we are walking into. We aren't children anymore, Alex. We know love can hurt, but now we both have the chance to know its pleasures. Together, it's possible. We'd be fools not to at least try.'

'Bohdi,' Alex tried to inject, but he wasn't done.

'No. I'm not finished,' said Bohdi. 'Alex Mason, I love you. You are what makes me whole. You are what I have been searching for. You aren't the only one who has been walking around afraid. I get it. But I love you. Do you hear me? I love you and I will do whatever it takes to win your heart.'

He stopped, took a deep breath, and then stared at her.

'Well?' he asked.

'Oh, am I allowed to speak now?'

Alex couldn't stop from teasing him. Her heart was singing. He loved her! He wanted them to take the chance on love, on life. Bohdi didn't look as amused.

'Seriously?'

'I'm sorry, I was kidding.' Alex reached over and wrapped her arms around his waist. 'I love you too, Bohdi Vonn. I was about to come and tell you. If you're willing to take the risk, then so am I.' She looked deep into his glistening eyes of blue. 'I've always loved you, even when I didn't want to. Even in the darkest hours, my heart always belonged to you.'

Bohdi responded, his eyes pleading. 'You worshipped a boy, Alex, but I need to know you can love me now. A man. This imperfect man, standing before you, desperate to love the woman you have become.'

'I do, Bohdi. I thought I could deny it, but it was foolish to think I could. I didn't need to go heli-skiing with you, I wanted to. I didn't want to admit it, but it doesn't make it any less true. I'm tired of pretending I don't love you. I don't want to waste any more time. We have done that long enough.'

Bohdi cradled her face in his strong hands. The warmth of his touch radiated throughout her whole body. His eyes glistened as he spoke. 'Really?'

It was one word, but Alex knew he was asking so much more.

'Really,' she responded.

Alex felt their tears join as Bohdi brought her lips to his, gently kissing her. It was perfect. A promise of a love and a chance at healing. Together.

EPILOGUE

The stars twinkled between flakes of snow that danced in the moonlight. Everyone was gathered together at the top of Centre Run to begin the annual Torchlight Parade.

Years ago, her father had suggested the idea as a tribute to loved ones lost. People had been so enamored of the idea that many came back to the resort solely for the parade.

Bohdi was lighting the torches as Alex organized the procession. She was pleased to see that Cal had come back. He looked so much better since RG had stopped their pursuit of Talisman and selling his share of the resort to Bohdi. It was like the weight of the world had been lifted from his shoulders.

Alex skied across the slope to Bohdi.

'You're getting pretty good at lighting those,' said Alex.

'I figure I'd better practice up if we are going to be spending two months every year in Fiji,' he laughed.

'Good point. Although I've never doubted your ability to heat things up.'

Bohdi passed off the last torch, then pulled Alex close, her skis between his. 'Don't tempt me, woman. I'll be happy to start a fire here. I don't care who's watching.'

'I believe you.' Alex laughed out loud. She no longer fought to hide her emotions. Being with Bohdi had allowed her to remember who she was. It was absolutely freeing.

With a promise of far more wicked things later, Bohdi gave her a kiss and skied over to the front of the parade.

They began the descent and Alex marvelled at the beauty of it all. With all the lights to the hill shut off, a quiet darkness spilled over the resort. All she could see was the snaking line of torches making their way down the run. The procession was a long one. It was a beautiful, but poignant, reminder that everyone has a story of loss.

When they finally reached the bottom, Alex skied back over to Bohdi's side. Their group created a large circle. As each person called out the name of their loved one lost, the group echoed that name.

Bohdi shared Ben's name and Alex shared her father's, then as a whole, the circle lowered their torches to be extinguished in the snow.

Alex looked over at Bohdi and then bumped her hip to his. He turned and looked down at her.

She ran her arm through his. 'I'm a lucky woman.'

Bohdi popped out of his skis and moved to stand before Alex. He twirled a loose strand of blonde hair that had escaped her braid.

'I'm the lucky one. I finally won gold. It was never a medal I needed. It was you.'

Manufactured by Amazon.ca
Bolton, ON

10219594R00096